D1564449

WWW.BEWAREORMONSTERS.COM

PRAISE FOR JEREMY ROBINSON

"[*Hunger* is] a wicked step-child of King and Del Toro. Lock your windows and bolt your doors. [Robinson, writing as] Jeremiah Knight, imagines the post-apocalypse like no one else."

—The Novel Blog

"Robinson writes compelling thrillers, made all the more entertaining by the way he incorporates aspects of pop culture into the action."

—Booklist

"*Project 731* is a must. Jeremy Robinson just keeps getting better with every new adventure and monster he creates."

—Suspense Magazine

"Robinson is known for his great thrillers, and [with *XOM-B*] he has written a novel that will be in contention for various science fiction awards at the end of the year. Robinson continues to amaze with his active imagination."

—Booklist

"Robinson puts his distinctive mark on Michael Crichton territory with [*Island 731*], a terrifying present-day riff on *The Island of Dr. Moreau*. Action and scientific explanation are appropriately proportioned, making this one of the best *Jurassic Park* successors."

—Publisher's Weekly
Starred Review

"[Jeremy Robinson's *SecondWorld* is] a brisk thriller with neatly timed action sequences, snappy dialogue and the ultimate sympathetic figure in a badly burned little girl with a fighting spirit... The Nazis are determined to have the last gruesome laugh in this efficient doomsday thriller."

—Kirkus Reviews

"Jeremy Robinson is the next James Rollins."

—Chris Kuzneski,
NY Times bestselling author of
The Einstein Pursuit

AN ANTARKTOS NOVELLA

THE LAST VALKYRIE

JEREMY ROBINSON
AND TORI PAQUETTE

Visit Jeremy Robinson on the World Wide Web at:
www.bewareofmonsters.com

Visit Tori Paquette on the World Wide Web at:
www.boldbrightbeautiful.com

ALSO BY JEREMY ROBINSON

THE LAST VALKYRIE

INTRODUCTION

I get a lot of requests for sequels for all my novels and series, but one stands out above the rest: The Last Hunter/Antarktos Universe. I have resisted for a long time, because I felt my time with Solomon (other than his recent appearance in *Project Legion*) had come to a very satisfying closure. That said, when it came time to put out *The Last Hunter Collected Edition*, I included a short story featuring Solomon's daughters, Aquila and Norah.

But over the years, I have resisted visiting Antarktos again, because my time there has come to a close. At the same time, the girl who started babysitting my children (Aquila, Solomon and Norah) was growing into an amazing writer. As she prepared for college at age 17, she was discussing her options for a summer job, and I realized we were in the perfect position to help each other.

Like the character of Solomon, who is based on my son, Aquila and Norah are based on my daughters, and there are few people who know them as well as "Tornado". So I presented her with the idea of her summer job being a visit to Antarktos with Aquila and Norah. She accepted, and here we are, back on the thawed continent, with the daughters of Solomon, cresties, the underworld, the Nephilim and a few amazing surprises!

I'm very excited for my readers to return to Antarktos, and to introduce them to Tori's writing, which I've had the pleasure of seeing improve over the years. If you enjoy your trip to Antarktos, would like to return and want to support Tori's first published book, please post a review on Amazon or Goodreads when you're done. Every one helps a lot!

Thank you!

—Jeremy Robinson

For the real Solomon,
who inspired an empire his sisters could inherit
...as his fictional daughters.
—Jeremy Robinson

For Norah and Aquila Robinson,
who have shown me that you don't
have to be big to be brave.
—Tori Paquette

THE KINGDOM OF ANTARKTOS

The Earth's crust has shifted. Antarctica moved to the equator, resulting in mass destruction around the world. At the center of this catastrophe, a boy named Solomon, the Last Hunter, rose to power in the re-christened *Antarktos*. Through his courage and strength, Solomon cleansed the land of its evil breed of half-human, half-demons, known as the Nephilim. He also freed the many people who were enslaved to the Nephilim, as hunters. A new civilization now thrives on Antarktos under Solomon's reign as King, providing a home to those who survived the global destruction. But some Nephilim still lie in wait under the surface, hiding in the caverns and tunnels of the underworld. They bide their time, plotting the King's destruction. With Solomon off fighting monsters in another realm, the Nephilim see their opportunity to take what he holds most dear...

1

My sister, Aquila, shouts loudly enough to wake the whole jungle as she dashes ahead, darting back and forth between the trees. I catch glimpses of her, slipping in and out of the green, a forest specter. Effortless. She turns around and waves her arms at me. "You're as slow as a one-legged turkuin!"

A really annoying specter.

I glare at her, but she's already off and running again. She's too focused on slashing vines with her sword. Of course, she still had time to compare me to one of the dumbest creatures in Antarktos: the turkuin, which is essentially half turkey, half penguin. The clever name for their breed is compliments of my father, Solomon, the King of Antarktos.

Zuh, our caretaker, looks back at me and slows her pace. I make no effort to catch up, but soon we're walking side by side. She takes shorter strides with her dark, lanky legs so that my short ones can keep up. It's annoying, actually. I hold my chin high and ignore her until she speaks.

"You and I can spend some time working on your fighting skills this evening." Zuh is a hunter from the old days, before the Nephilim were defeated. She is our stalwart defender, but once existed in darkness, corrupted by the Nephilim—as was my father, for a time. She's brought us out into the jungle to train us. Again. She swings the chain of her weapon idly, the curved knives at both ends glittering with sunlight. It's called a kusarigama, and it's always ready to whip out and slice her enemies.

"We'll send Aquila off on a hunt so she won't—"

"Nope. Thanks." I grit my teeth and stare straight ahead.

"Norah." Zuh sighs. "You are capable. Despite what you believe."

I stay silent. What does she want me to say? *Yeah, I know, I just don't want to. Leave me alone.* I can feel her looking at me, and I make sure to hold my mouth steady, my jaw firm. I'm nothing if not resolute.

Zuh smacks at her arm and curses. "I miss my days in the underground sometimes. No bloodsucking insects."

I watch as the bug she didn't catch flies away, fat with her blood.

She looks at me again, then scans the jungle up ahead, searching for Aquila. There's nothing to see, but the twang of my sister's blade, carving a path through the underbrush, is easy enough to hear. "If she keeps up that racket, she's going to scare away our supper." Zuh clips the knife back to its place on the chain wrapped around her body and jogs ahead.

When I'm sure she's not looking, I let myself relax. My shoulders sag, and although I'm ashamed to admit it, my lip trembles. But only a little. I look down at the hammer swinging from my hand, the hammer I named *Smite*. Not because I liked the name, but because my mother did...and because I wanted my weapon to sound as fierce as my sister's. It's a small replica of my mother's hammer, modeled after Thor's legendary hammer, Mjölnir. She likes to remind me of the hammer's ferocity, and how she used it to overcome the so-called 'gods,' who were really Nephilim— half-demon, half-human cross-bred monsters. When she's done, my father likes to jump in, reminding me of the evil of the Nephilim, and how they kidnapped humans and broke them, molding them into hunters who carried out their heinous plans. While the retelling has become annoying,

I have trouble picturing people like my parents and Zuh being broken, or turned evil, but he tells the story with unwavering conviction. And despite the story's end—that the Nephilim were defeated—he tells me to be careful in the wilderness of Antarktos, and that I shouldn't go underground without a caretaker, because I might meet a surviving Nephilim in hiding. What he's too blind to see is that I already know that, and I have no interest. I'd rather be in the gardens at home, drawing the birds and insects that flourish there.

I finger the sketchpad hidden in the pouch around my waist. Zuh would kill me if she knew I'd brought it. *We're here to train, Norah,* she'd say in her best disappointed voice, which sounds a lot more like an irritated tiger. *You've got to learn to defend yourself, and to hunt. The animals you draw will not fill your belly, or come to your rescue.*

"Alright, princesses," Zuh says, leading Aquila back toward me, mocking us with the term. Aquila bristles. She'd much rather be called *hunter.* But I hear what Aquila misses—respect for the daughters of Solomon, the Last Hunter, the King of Antarktos. "Time to stop and practice some self-defense skills."

Aquila spins on her heel and runs back into the clearing where Zuh has stopped. I amble in and take a look around. It's bright here. Bright and cool. When the Earth's crust shifted, Antarktos—once called Antarctica—became a tropical place, much like Brazil was supposed to be. Wind stirs the trees and dances violently with the flapping leaves. I'll have to factor in the direction of the wind when I throw Smite, and the glare of the sun on its metal surface, which could cause painful, blinding distractions on either side...

Stop, I tell myself. *You are not a fighter. Not anymore.*

Aquila whips her sword out in front of her, the blade uncurling. It is a Nephilim-made weapon that used to belong to our grandfather, the infamous Lieutenant Ninnis, who nearly destroyed all of civilization when he was possessed by the spirit of Nephil. Inhabited by the first of the Nephilim, Ninnis attempted to lead the half-demons in conquering the world, and he nearly instituted a new world order. Thanks to my father—and Ninnis—Nephil failed. Ninnis's sword—named 'Strike' by Ninnis—has a flexible blade that can curl down to a tiny size, easily hidden. It's perfect for traversing the under-ground. With a skillful flick of the wrist, the full-sized blade can spring out at an unsuspecting enemy.

With her light brown hair whipping around her face and her beaded leathers tied about her shoulders and her waist, Aquila truly looks like a warrior princess. Her blue eyes glint with as much power as the sword in her hands. At age sixteen, she's four years older than me, and four years bolder. Most of the time she acts like she doesn't have a care in the world.

Without a word, Zuh swings her kusarigama at Aquila, the knife hurtling toward my sister's head. Aquila blocks it with a flick of the sword, then twists the chain around her blade and pulls Zuh toward her. Zuh sees the tactic coming and hurls the other end of her chain, with its matching curved blade, at Aquila's feet. The chain wraps tightly, and Zuh tugs, pulling Aquila to the ground. The knife leaves a laceration on Aquila's calf, and her eyes burn with embarrassment.

"Anticipate your opponent's next move." In Zuh's voice there is a hint of mocking laughter, but her fierce eyes show that she is dead serious. "Or you will die."

I shake my head and turn away. Aquila's problem is her passion. She attacks without thought and doesn't plan ahead. It's all about the glory of the fight and not about the skill and precision it takes to win.

"Norah's turn." Zuh turns to where I stood, blades raised. But I have already disappeared into the forest. From the shade of the trees, I watch her look around the clearing and sigh. "Norah?" She looks at Aquila and mumbles, "I don't know how your father expects me to train you two…"

I lean back against a tree trunk and slide to the ground. The canopy above me shimmers and sways, diamond-shaped leaves overlapping into a pattern of sunlight and shadows. I pull out my sketchbook and charcoals and start to draw, the slivers of light and dark on the page at war with each other.

Something rustles nearby. I freeze and look around. How could we have not scared away all the animals with the noise we've been making?

But there it is—a little brown creature with big black eyes and tiny paws, staring up at me.

"Hello," I whisper.

It tilts its head, whiskers twitching. The creature creeps closer and sets its front paws on the ground. It's about a foot-and-a-half long and looks like a large guinea pig with a bean for a tail. But I recognize it. It's an agouti, a tropical creature that lost its home in Brazil and probably came to Antarktos with any South Americans that survived the Earth's crustal shift. It's just one of hundreds of refugee species now calling Antarktos home—including humanity—all adding to the bio-diversity of a continent thought to be lifeless since Antarctica froze. Now, a huge variety of creatures live here. And more than just your typical jungle animals. Creatures that had been living in underground tunnels for thousands of years have come to the surface, including dinosaurs, strange birds, exotic predators and who knows what else. Compared to most, the agouti in front of me is harmless.

"What are you up to, little guy?"

He chirps at me.

"Want me to draw a picture of you?"

He chirps again, several short squeals in a row, and lays on the forest floor, looking up at me. As if he's waiting.

Awed, I flip to a new sheet of paper. Little guys like this don't usually wander close to people or really to anything bigger than them—especially in the dangerous land of Antarktos. I start to sketch him while he stays calm and still, only his whiskers moving.

The moment is perfect until forceful footsteps disturb the ground behind me.

I jump up and whirl around, hammer in hand. But it's only Aquila.

She frowns at me, one hand on her hip. "What are you doing out here? You should be training."

"I have better things to do." I look around, but my new agouti friend must have heard the intruder, too. He darted away before I could say good-bye.

"What was that thing you were talking to? A rat?"

I glare. "It was an agouti. And you scared him away."

"Well, sorry to interrupt."

She's not sorry, and we both know it.

"C'mon, Norah. We get to hang out with Zuh! No parents. No rules. Just us and the forest and our weapons." Her eyes gleam. While she is duty bound as my older sister to act impatient with me, I know she's just eager for me to share in her fun. "Maybe we'll even get to fight a Nephilim!"

"Yeah, that would be fantastic." I sigh when Aquila nods, either choosing to ignore, or not hearing, the thick slathering of sarcasm coating my words. "Tell Zuh I'm coming."

When night descends, we set up camp. We plan to sleep in the trees, hammocks slung over sturdy branches. The only wandering creature that might pose a threat to us is a cresty, formally called a *Cryolophosaurus*. They're red and green dinosaurs, averaging twenty feet in length, though some reach thirty. And they like to snack on large prey. In the past, they even killed and ate Nephilim. Today, though, they're mostly friendly and domesticated, thanks to my father's connection with them. But there are still wild cresties, and they wouldn't think twice about eating us.

And then there is the unknown. Antarktos is a mostly unexplored continent. You never know what you'll find in the jungles, mountains and rivers, and I'd prefer to be high above any predators seeking a nocturnal meal. Hammocks are comfortable compared to sleeping on the ground, too, so I'm not complaining.

After we've selected a few closely gathered trees, shimmied up the trunks and tied the makeshift beds in their heights, we start our next task: building a fire. It's a skill Zuh has taught us before, but it's one that's always good to practice. We sit around our pile of wood, and Aquila takes a turn striking the flint and steel.

She squints, trying and failing again and again. Her strikes are too impatient. I want to correct her, but I won't give Zuh the satisfaction.

Finally, Aquila pauses. "This is stupid." She drops the flint and steel in front of Zuh. "Can't you tell us one of your stories?" She perks up. "The gravestone! Tell us that one!"

Zuh rolls her eyes and picks up the flint and steel. It takes her less than three strikes to get a spark going. Air flows from her pursed lips, fueling the fire, which spreads and blooms, bright and yellow.

"Come on, Zuh!" Aquila begs.

Zuh settles back, hands on her bare belly. "After the last battle with the Nephilim, many gravestones were built for the soldiers and hunters who had fallen." Despite Zuh's typically strict tone, I can see the sadness in her eyes. "There were so many bodies that not all of them could be recovered and identified. During the chaos that follows any battle, I returned to the underworld in pursuit of fleeing Nephilim. It was not a task assigned to me—just something I had to do. There will come a time in your life when you will have to do something like this, too." Zuh looks long at Aquila, then at me. "Where you will know in your gut that you alone have a mission to complete, no matter what it costs. Life is a series of trials, some more deadly than others, but this is why we train. The body and mind grow strong in tandem."

Something twists in my stomach at her words. Her tone is dark and serious. I think I like the snappy, irritated Zuh better than this.

Zuh stares into the jungle canopy above us, remembering. The fire, crackling now, lights her dark face and high cheekbones from below. "They thought I was among the dead, and so they built an empty grave for me. When I returned—before I visited anyone else—I went to the cemetery to mourn the fallen. And I found my own name." Zuh laughs a little, but I can tell it's a laugh to cover up sadness.

"Of course, I went to your parents immediately, who had been mourning me. Your father...has always been affection-ate, but I never thought your mother would be happy to see me after the things I did. The harsh words we spoke. The violence..."

Aquila grins. "Like when you thought *you* should marry Dad, and not her?"

"He told you about that, huh?" Zuh smirks. "I still think I would have been a smart choice. And that we should have had a rematch."

Hunters battling it out for marriage rights. I shake my head at the strange custom from the old days.

"Did you find many Nephilim?" Aquila asks. "After the battle?"

Zuh nods. "Some gatherers. Breeders. Various species who hadn't been involved on the battle's front lines. The warriors—the biggest, highest-ranking Nephilim—were all but gone after the battle. And of course, some species of Nephilim are harder to find—"

"Shifters," Aquila says, garnering a nod from Zuh.

We've been taught about the Nephilim for as long as I can remember, which is pretty far back. Shifters can take on the form of any person with just a taste of their blood.

The idea of being underground sounds less and less appealing to me the more Zuh talks about it. Suddenly I feel very thankful for the hammocks and the trees. The shush of wind through the leaves around us, smelling of jungle flowers and fruit, must be paradise compared to the dank underworld.

Zuh stares at the fire for a long moment, eyes burning with something I don't recognize. Then she asks me—again—if I'd like to train.

"I'm tired," I say.

It's an excuse, and she knows it. Her eyebrows raise, dark and furry like her hair. Sometimes I'd like to tell her it's hard to take her seriously with her pom-pom of hair—which my father calls a 'fro' when he's teasing her—but I know she wouldn't take it kindly.

When Aquila stands, Zuh says, "If you don't want to train with me, Aquila could use the practice."

Aquila looks like she's been pinched. "Uhh, no. I gotta go number two. I'll be back in a few minutes."

Zuh sighs, but obliges. I can tell she's annoyed that Aquila used the old American slang—that odd term 'number two'—which she must have learned from father's military friends. I watch as Aquila bounds down the slope.

As soon as she's out of Zuh's line of sight, she runs in the other direction.

I wonder what she's doing that she doesn't want Zuh to know about. Probably off to kill a small animal so we have fresh meat for dinner. Of course she has to do it herself. Quil can't be anything less than self-sufficient. I snort and shake my head.

"What?" Zuh asks.

"Just thinking about what would happen if a bird thought your puff of hair was a nest."

I was right. She doesn't take it kindly. She glares at me and swings her bladed chain in my direction. I throw my hammer and pin the knife to the ground.

"I told you: you're capable," she grumbles, jerking the chain out from under Smite. She swings at me again, but my hammer's on the ground, and my mind blanks in fear. I stumble backward and fall on my butt. The chain hurtles over my head, and I feel the breeze in my hair, tugging at my dark blonde wisps. I feel my face flush as I scramble to my feet and grab Smite.

"Enough," I say. "I told you, I don't want to fight."

"You froze." Zuh tugs on the chain and catches the curved blade as it snaps back. "That could be the death of you."

I turn and stalk away as if I don't care, but my pale skin flames all the way up to my hairline. I shimmy up a tree and lie in my hammock so she won't see.

Ten minutes go by, and I hear Zuh pacing beneath me, mumbling. "Where is she? Not even a Warrior takes that long..."

She's gone, I think. *And you didn't even notice. Good job, Zuh. You're quite the hunter.*

I sit up in the hammock and dangle my legs over the edge. Zuh looks up at me. "I'm going to go check on Aquila."

I don't feel my expression change, but Zuh is observant enough to spot subtle changes.

Her forehead wrinkles in annoyance. "What?"

"You won't find her."

Zuh crosses her arms, annoyance growing, but I see fear in her eyes. "Why?"

"She ran off in the other direction. She lied to you."

Zuh squints up at me. "You not telling me is an equal offense. Whatever punishment she faces, you will share in it." She turns to the jungle behind her, looking through the trees. "Where?" There is stifled panic in her voice.

"That way." I point to where I'd seen Aquila fade into the distance.

"I'm going after her." Zuh already has her hands on her kusarigama, prepared to strike and break whatever gets in her way. "You stay here."

"I'm not planning on—"

Zuh is already running through the trees.

In seconds, I'm alone.

The night darkens, the quarter moon's light not powerful enough to pierce through the lush canopy. Even more distressing, Zuh hasn't returned. I strain my ears, listening for something, anything—footfalls, the crackle of leaves, voices. All I hear are cooing night noises and the occasional shrill call of nocturnal animals. Fear paralyzes me. If I move, perhaps *I* will be heard, and the high-pitched, hungry cries will then be directed at me. I don't think I could even move to defend myself.

Where are you, Zuh?

And what if they're injured—or worse?

I can't bring myself to think it. What if they need me? Should I search for them? My heart pounds, an accelerating drumbeat. I begin to feel warm and dizzy, muscles twitching as adrenaline rushes through my body. I've got to do something or I'm going to pass out.

I leap from the hammock, descend through the branches below and drop to the ground, landing in a crouch. The hammer at my side anchors me. I take a deep breath and set off through the dark, aiming for the point where I last saw Zuh.

INTERLUDE 1 OF 2

Aquila Vincent, princess of Antarktos, eldest daughter of King Solomon, felt exhilarated by the fresh forest air. It smelled of green leaves, layers of decay, animal droppings and warm bodies. This was her chance. She would trap an animal and show Zuh she was capable of fending for herself. She would earn the right to be a hunter—to no longer need a guardian in the jungle, to be able to fight her own battles and survive her own way. She had expressed these desires to her parents on many occasions in the past, but they always requested patience, and they spoke of dangers unseen. As much as she loved and even admired her parents, the strongest and most deadly hunters in all of Antarktos, she believed their stories were exaggerated to keep her afraid, and close. They didn't understand her need for space. For freedom.

She followed the animal scent, bending close to the ground, sniffing like a dog. She could smell where animals had stepped and where they had marked their territory. The more pungent, the more recent. And the odor stinging her nose was very recent. These were all skills she'd learned from the women in her life: her mother, Kainda, her 'aunts' Em, Mira and Kat, and of course, from Zuh. Because Zuh had continued to live underground for long after the Nephilim had been defeated, and because she knew which areas were safe and which were more likely to harbor the surviving creatures, she led most of the underground expeditions. When Kainda had time and wasn't off fighting by Solomon's side, she took the girls out on shorter lessons in the woods. This time, though, Kainda had stayed home to manage the country while Solomon was away, fighting for 'all dimensions of Earth'—whatever that meant— and she'd sent the girls off with Zuh.

Aquila sighed.

Sometimes it felt like her father was always in demand. Everyone admired him; everyone wanted his help. He was incredibly strong, both of body and of soul. He could control the continent of Antarktos—its land, water and air—with his will. He was the first and only natural born Antarctican before the global shift, and the Last Hunter, destined to be the vessel of Nephil—who had intended to use Solomon's vast power to conquer the world. Yet Solomon had been strong enough to resist and defeat Nephil. Aquila had heard the story more times than she could count—not from her father, because he was too humble for that, but from everyone who talked about his deeds in awed voices. Her mother, her fellow hunters, the people in the street—everyone knew what Solomon had done, and everyone admired him for it.

Aquila wondered how she could ever measure up to the standard he had set. At age thirteen, he had been broken and then come back to himself, escaping the Nephilim's control. She was sixteen and she had done what? Nothing. No one talked about her in the streets. No one admired her. No one asked her for her help or her advice. She had not conquered any Nephilim, and she had not gone on any magnificent adventures. She didn't have any powers.

Aquila stopped beside a brook, crouching down on the gravelly earth and the outcropping of stones. She drew out the rope she'd hidden in her pouch and tied a knot with vengeance. She would show them what she could do. Even if she didn't have any powers, she was a born fighter. She would track down animals, and then, she would track down Nephilim.

She would cleanse Antarktos of those evil creatures, and people would revere her name, just like her father's. And even better, her father would be proud of her, too.

The air shifted, bringing a new scent with it, but Aquila, busy tying a noose, fixing the spring pole and baiting her trap, failed to notice.

"Going to catch you," she muttered. "And then we're going to eat you. You won't even see this coming."

"Just like you didn't see me coming?"

Aquila jumped to her feet, whipping Strike open. She relaxed when she saw it was only Zuh. "Zuh, I—"

"Decided to take a little 'alone time?'" Zuh's voice sounded mocking. She flicked a hand, waving a large bloodsucking insect away from where it hovered around her pouf of hair.

"I'm catching dinner," Aquila said. She tried to sound confident, but even she could hear the guilt in her voice.

Zuh shook her head. "Foolish. Don't you know what's out in the jungle, child?"

Her derisive tone made Aquila frown. "I'm *not* a child. I'm a *hunter*."

Zuh's laugh sounded like a bark. "A hunter? You're still a little girl."

"I have trained," Aquila said, voice heated. "*You* said I'm doing well."

"I lied to boost your confidence." Zuh sneered, eyes hard. She picked up a jagged rock, which was probably six inches in diameter, and began passing it from hand to hand. "You're not good enough to be out here on your own."

Aquila fought the urge to turn and run. She couldn't show Zuh any weakness. But she'd never seen her this angry. Had Aquila known how sneaking off would affect her guardian, she'd have never left.

Stand your ground, she told herself. *Show her you're strong enough.*

"You taught me everything I know!" Aquila yelled. "If there's anything wrong with my skills, it's because I had a bad teach—"

The rock whizzed through the air and hit Aquila smack in the stomach, stopping her words short. She fell to the ground with an *oomph*.

Aquila stood up on shaky legs, drawing Strike once more. "You need me to prove my fighting skills?"

Zuh licked her lips and smirked at Aquila.

Aquila felt fury rise up in her chest. "Fine." She swung Strike around, swinging the flat side of the blade at Zuh's head. But it never reached its target. Zuh grabbed it with an open hand and wrenched it down and away.

Aquila was stunned. Strike was supernaturally sharp. Zuh was lucky her fingers hadn't been severed. "Zuh!"

If Zuh felt any pain from gripping the sword, she showed no sign. Instead, she picked up another rock and flung it at Aquila's head. Aquila twisted to the side, but it struck her in the ear. She could feel warm blood dripping down the side of her face.

"You still have much to learn, girl." Zuh's voice was menacing and dark.

Aquila stared at her, not understanding. "What was that for?" She held out her hand, covered in blood from the side of her head.

"Your first real lesson," Zuh mocked. "Isn't the pain wonderful?"

Aquila glared and then charged. Strike connected with Zuh's shoulder, opening up a small and shallow gash. As she drew back to prepare for her next blow, she stopped short, eyes locked on the fresh wound.

Blood pulsed from Zuh's shoulder and hand.

Purple blood.

"Zuh?" Aquila asked, confused and distracted.

Then her mentor struck again. This time the blow collided with Aquila's hand, and Strike skittered across the ground, landing fifteen feet behind them.

Aquila turned to retrieve it, but Zuh tackled her, wrestling her to the ground. She sat on top of Aquila, straddling her waist.

"I never cared for you much." Zuh leaned into Aquila's face, breath hot and rough on her skin. Aquila pulled back, struggling, her scalp digging into the ground. Zuh pushed down on her collarbone with one hand—the hand not covered in purple blood. "Neither do your parents. You're so little. So insignificant. Such a disappointment." Zuh caught the bloodsucking insect still floating around her head and shoved it into her mouth, sucking it dry and licking her lips. "Mmm. I taste blood."

Aquila screamed as Zuh's fingernails dug into her skin.

Another voice yelled from farther away. "Aquila? Is that you?" The voice sounded panicked—and strangely like Zuh's.

Zuh looked up into the woods and sneered at what she saw. "Well. Looks like we've got company."

Taking advantage of the distraction, Aquila kicked her legs and twisted, wresting herself free from Zuh's weight. She stood up just in time to see another Zuh run into the clearing.

Breathing heavily, throat raw, Aquila looked back and forth between the two women. The first Zuh, the Zuh with purple blood dripping down her arm, gave the new Zuh a mocking glare.

The second Zuh stared at the first, aghast. "Aquila, stand back!"

Aquila shuffled back, confused, still staring in shock. Which one was Zuh? If the first woman wasn't Zuh—then who had she been fighting?

"I know what you are," the second Zuh hissed.

"And I know you, Zuh of the Greeks." Evil Zuh laughed. She spread her arms wide. "I suppose you'd like to defend your incapable charge?"

The second Zuh whipped a chain free and swung a knife directly into the first Zuh's chest.

The first Zuh laughed again, louder, eyes glowing with delight and hate. She pulled the knife out of her chest. Purple blood dribbled down, and then her dark, stained skin opened up, pulling back and away.

Something inside was clawing loose, like a chick fighting against an egg. Only this was much bigger. Skin ripped away. Exposed muscle covered in red scales emerged, freeing itself from the outer layer that had been disguised as Zuh, moving as if it had its own mind.

Aquila watched in horror as the muscled, morphing creature grew, buckling, swaying, expanding and shedding its Zuh-skin, until it stood ten feet tall. Huge muscles bubbled underneath the glistening red scales that coated the thing's skin. A grimace exposed double rows of teeth. Two horns punched through the forehead and grew into six-inch hooks.

The woman who Aquila now knew was the real Zuh swore. "A shifter."

Aquila felt a tremor of fear and excitement shiver across her skin. A Nephilim. This was her first real sighting. She ran for Strike, scooping it up off the forest floor.

The real Zuh stood bold before the much larger creature, her dark brown eyes burning with fire...and recognition. "Loki."

The creature grinned and bowed. "The harbinger of mass destruction and chaos on planet Earth."

"As I recall, you were the weaker of two twins bestowed with the same name. Your brother, the warrior, always made the Norse proud, whereas you... Where *have* you been hiding?" Zuh began to spin her blade, ready to attack. "And why are you attacking my ward?"

"That tiny girl?" Loki hissed. "Or should I call her *Princess?*"

Coming off his lips, the word sounded laughable. Aquila gripped the curled Strike tightly in her fist, preparing to attack—as soon as Zuh said she could come closer.

"Aquila, Princess of Antarktos, daughter of the King," Loki continued. "And what a king he is."

"What do you know about my father?" Aquila raised her voice.

Zuh shot her a look that said, *Shut up.*

The Nephilim's yellow eyes gleamed as he looked at the small girl below him. The sixteen-year-old princess was only five feet tall—half his size. He laughed. "You failed to fight a much smaller human form. Do you really want to fight me now?"

Aquila swelled up, pushing her chest out. Then she glared at Loki. "My father said the Nephilim were often thirty feet tall. You must be the runt of the litter."

The devilish creature sneered and took a heavy step toward her. The earth trembled beneath her feet, but she tamped down her fear and stood her ground.

Just one more step, she thought.

In one quick movement, before Zuh could stop her, Aquila snapped open Strike and drove it upward, deep into Loki's groin.

At first, she thought he howled. But a moment later she knew the truth: Loki was laughing.

Ecstatic with pleasure.

Aquila shivered and drew back her sword, covered in purple blood. She watched as thick purple ooze dripped down Loki's leg and matted against the thick red hair that grew in patches around his scaly skin.

Laughing, Loki crouched so that his head was level with Aquila's. "You're lucky I need you alive, little girl."

Aquila sliced Loki's face, a clean cut below his cheekbone. He leered at her as the blood trickled along the red skin. She watched, horrified, as the wound closed itself up, leaving only a purple stain on his face.

"Touch it. You'll see. It's healed."

If Aquila had been paying attention, she would have heard the delight in his voice, the anticipation, the deception. But she was in awe. She had never seen anything like this before. She reached out a hand to touch his face...

"Aquila! Stop!"

Aquila's hand froze in midair. She heard the unusual fear in Zuh's voice, and it frightened her. She stepped back as Zuh charged, chains swinging.

Zuh's blades danced violently around Loki's legs, but he batted them away like toothpicks. The cuts on his hands healed in seconds. Zuh swung one chain low, at Loki's legs, and one high, aiming for the top of Loki's head. But the distraction failed.

He reached up to grab the knife before it connected with his skull.

"Thought you could trick me?" he growled, as he loosened the chain wrapped around his legs. "I am the original trickster." He yanked the chain, which was looped tightly around Zuh's torso. It lifted her up into the air. She flailed, helpless, as he hurled her up high, and then brought her down to the ground with a crash.

Zuh got to her feet, but her legs shook. She pulled her chain back and whipped it toward Loki again. He caught it again and pulled with ferocity, knocking her down and dragging her along the ground. When she reached his feet, he twisted the chain, grinding it into her skin, where it wrapped around her body. Then she lurched forward with the end of the kusarigama she still had. The knife was aimed at his chest.

Before it reached him, he caught her wrist and bent it backward until it snapped. Zuh's eyes grew wide with pain. Her fingers went limp, dropping the knife. Loki grinned as he picked up both knives and stabbed them into either side of her thin body and then slammed his forehead into hers. Zuh fell to her knees, then slumped forward at Loki's feet.

In the dead silence that followed, Loki's double-rowed grin and bright yellow eyes craned to face Aquila.

She screamed.

Zuh twitched on the ground. Her hair was red with blood. Loki bent down and ran a finger through the hair, collecting blood and licking it off his finger.

"Zuh!" The scream turned into a sob.

The Nephilim turned to the little girl, whose emotions had unhinged her. "Your turn."

A hand barreled through the air toward her. A scream and a moment of intense pain, and then there was darkness.

2

Even in the warm humidity of the rainforest, I shiver. I don't know who or what is out here. I don't know where I'm going. And I can't see my feet well enough to avoid stepping on crackling leaves or snapping twigs. Occasionally a vibrant star will pierce through the thick foliage above me, but those bits of light are few and far between.

Every muscle in my body is rigid. I grip Smite with everything I have, but I feel it trembling against my side. I have to remind myself to breathe.

"Zuh?" I whisper.

The groan of wind against branches.

I shiver and try again. "Aquila?"

The leaves rub above me, a rasping sound like laughter.

I stop and squint at the forest around me. All I see are shadows upon shadows. My throat feels tight. Blood rushes through my body, making me dizzy. What if I pass out? Will they find me dead in the morning? Will there be anyone left to find me in the morning?

I feel tears prickling in my eyes, and that's when I force myself to stop.

You can't fall apart now, Norah. Breathe.

I breathe.

I let my heart slow.

And I listen harder.

"Zuh?" I call her name louder this time.

A moan.

That must be her!

At least, it's someone. I sniff the air like Aquila would, hoping to catch a whiff of something I recognize. And then

I do—but it's not the familiar scent of a person. It's the scent of blood.

Human.

...and something else.

I follow the smell, slowly at first, and then rushing, tripping over roots and rocks. But the smell gets stronger, and the moans continue.

The adrenaline has moved to the pit of my stomach, and it swims with nausea. The smell of blood is overpowering now, and with it comes the taste in my mouth: warm and sickening, the taste of fear and pain and of memories I've forced back.

And then I'm there, almost tripping over her body.

Zuh.

She's lying on the ground, and from what I can smell, there's blood everywhere.

"Oh, Zuh, oh—" I stop. Clutch my stomach. And I turn away just in time so that when I vomit, it doesn't land on her. Shaking, I wipe my mouth and turn back to kneel at her side. My quivering fingers find her pulse, throbbing at the base of her neck.

She's alive.

I breathe a sigh of relief.

I force myself to work past the overwhelming fear and think. What should I do? I struggle to think back on the things my parents—and Zuh—have taught me over the years. *Don't touch Nephilim blood. Cover your wounds. Stop the bleeding.*

Where is the wound? I move my hands across the ground until I find the deepest pool of blood and go from there. Her head. *Her head is bleeding.* That's bad.

But what am I supposed to do? I can't see anything. I need light...

Fire!

I rummage through the pouch on Zuh's belt and find a flint stone and steel. I just watched her do this; it shouldn't be too hard...

I hope.

I rustle together some dried leaves and broken branches from the forest floor and make a little heap with the leaves on top. Then I strike.

At first, my sweat and my shaking hands make striking the flint stone difficult. But after a few minutes, I get a spark. I blow on it gently, coaxing the leaves alight.

As the fire grows, I realize that it won't be long before all the branches are ash, and there will be nothing left to burn. I scramble to my feet and begin rummaging along the ground, which I can see much more clearly now.

That's when I notice the purple blood.

It's spattered across the leaves in thick globs, spread out over a wide circle on the forest floor. And it's pungent with a rotting animal smell.

The shock of the moment has passed, and I realize what this scent is. It's the scent of the Nephilim.

My stomach shivers again, threatening to hurl whatever sloshing, acidic remains are left. A Nephilim—at least one—attacked Zuh. And...Aquila.

Was Aquila here, too? I sniff the air, searching for her scent, but the combination of human and Nephilim blood is overpowering. Was she attacked? And if so...where is she? Aquila doesn't have the fighting skills—or the survival skills—that Zuh has. If whatever attacked Zuh got to her, Aquila's got to be...

I grip my hammer, fingers slick with sweat. I can't think like that. Not now—not while Zuh needs my help. I breathe deeply and focus on gathering more branches.

When I've gathered all the fallen branches within the small circle of light, I snap some low-hanging bits off the trees.

I discover quickly that these don't burn as well, because they hold moisture like any living plant. I could kick myself for not thinking of that sooner. Both Zuh and my mother have taught me that green branches will not do me much good. I search farther into the woods to collect broken branches, returning to keep the fire stoked.

The light eases some of my fear until I return to Zuh, lying crumpled on the ground. Her weapon is gone. Her shoulders look naked without the kusarigama wrapped around them. In the light, I can see her wound clearly. It's big—a three-inch gash in her scalp. The blood around the edges has congealed, but the center still oozes. Her normally dark face has grown pale. She's lost a lot of blood, and it's not stopping. The wound has to be closed up. But I don't have a needle and thread.

My heart stutters as I realize what I have to do. I look from the fire to Smite and back at Zuh.

The funny thing is, Zuh is the one who taught me how to cauterize a wound. She explained it, anyway—there was no demonstration. At the time, I was uninterested and even irritated that I had to learn such a useless skill. Now I wish she *had* given us a demonstration. What if I kill her? That much heat so close to her skull...

I take a deep breath and remove my hammer from its clip at my waist. It must be done. If I don't do it, she really could die. And Aquila isn't here to help me.

I kneel by the fire and put the head of the hammer into the flames. Thinking back on our cauterization lesson, I can hear Zuh's voice in my head: *Not too hot.*

How hot is 'too hot,' Zuh? I wonder.

I can't touch Smite to test its temperature, so I watch and wait. When it begins to glow red, I yank it out. *Too hot.* After a couple of minutes, the glowing metal has dimmed. Good enough—I hope.

I crouch by Zuh's head. My hands shake as I bring the metal near her bloody scalp. "I'm sorry, Zuh," I whisper, and then the metal touches skin.

She groans, eyelids fluttering, but she doesn't return to consciousness. I pull the hammer away. Then I hear myself crying, but it's like I'm listening to someone far away. The wound looks darker and thicker, but it's still wet. I press the hammer to her head again, just for a second, and pull it back. She gives a small moan.

With each touch, the wound grows darker. After a few touches, I stop and squint. It doesn't look like it's bleeding anymore. And she's breathing. I sit back on my heels and drop Smite on the ground.

That's when I start to really cry. Snot and tears cool my face. I want to curl up into a tiny part of myself, deep down where no one can see, where I'm not sitting in the dark, covered in blood, fighting for my friend's life and feeling more than incompetent. Feeling afraid.

"I'm not good enough, Zuh," I sob. "I can't do this. I'm not strong enough. I haven't trained enough. Don't make me do this alone. Please." My breath skids in my throat, uncomfortable and raw. "I'm so scared."

Fear—a feeling that neither Zuh nor my mother would ever admit they experienced. To a hunter, fear is shameful. Hunters are strong. Hunters know what to do. Hunters know how to face danger, how to fight, how to survive.

How to die well.

But I am not a hunter. And I don't want to be. I never want to face danger again, to feel so helpless and weak.

You are weak.

The voice slithers into my thoughts, cold and rasping, the same voice I hear every night as I fall asleep.

I have seen your mind. You are not what they think you are. You are...powerless. Afraid.

My eyes snap open, letting in the forest's darkness once more. The firelight wavers in the leaves. The wind purrs, and Zuh breathes lightly. No one else is here. The voice is just a memory.

My heart rattles against my ribcage like an inmate at the bars of his cell, and I force myself to breathe again.

I look over at Zuh and at the wound on her head. Knowing I caused that dark burn, the red, melted, unrecognizable flesh—it makes me feel ill. But I think she would be proud. Maybe even grateful. The thought makes me smile a little.

I'm not powerless. I can do something. I may have just saved Zuh's life—and I'm going to do whatever it takes to make sure she stays alive. Tonight she needs a guard, and that's what I'll be.

I settle back against a nearby tree and look out over the forest and the fire, eyes open for any predators. I will be her guard. I will...

When my eyes open again, it's daylight.

The air is sticky and humid.

And someone's hand is on my shoulder.

3

"Norah." Zuh's voice is raspy and unnatural. "Wake up."

I jolt upright, already reaching for Smite. "What? What is it?"

"You have to find her." Zuh's eyes are huge in her dark face, which is stained with sweat and dried blood. She half-sits, half-lies on the ground in front of me, one hand pressed tightly against her side. She looks too weak to stand.

I blink away the grogginess. I fell asleep when I should have been keeping watch. "I'm sorry, Zuh, I'm so—" I look her over, and guilt settles over me. In the daylight, I can see blood all along her torso, and I realize she has more than just a head wound. She's been stabbed, in the side. On *both* sides. The hand she reached out with to me hangs strangely at the end of her arm. Broken.

"Norah. You have to find your sister. You have to go. Now."

"Go where?"

"Loki took her. He's got to be—" Zuh looks out into the woods, eyes searching feverishly. She looks like she's gone mad—her usually fluffy hair has been pressed into awkward angles, held stiff with blood. Sweat gleams on her face. She looks frantic.

"Zuh, you don't look good..." It dawns on me—I never made an antiseptic poultice for her wound. I bet bacteria are having a field day in her skull. I reach out and touch her forehead. I was right. It's burning. "You've got to lie down and let me—"

"No!" Zuh shrieks, voice breaking. "She's going to die. Don't you understand? They've taken Aquila."

Aquila.

Zuh's words catch up to my exhausted brain. I stare out into the woods, eyes searching like Zuh's, looking for her. Aquila's been taken. By Loki...a Nephilim.

A shifter.

I'm paralyzed.

"Norah. Look at me," Zuh pleads.

I drag my eyes back to her face.

"She needs you."

I stare at the blood etched into the creases of her face, the dark hollows under her eyes. "You need me," I say, but even to me the words sound like a question, like a frightened plea to not have to hunt down a Nephilim.

Zuh takes a rattling breath, her forehead creased as though she's searching for words. Then she puts her good hand on my knee—a shaking hand, I note. My hands are shaking, too.

"I know you've had a hard time this year...even though I don't know why. You...haven't been yourself."

I look away, suddenly feeling vulnerable and exposed.

"But if you don't go..." Zuh squeezes my knee. "I can't go. And your father's far away. Too far away. We're not expected back for weeks. Help is *not* coming. You are the only one who has a chance at finding her."

I wish she would say what we're both thinking: *if she's still alive.*

Zuh slumps onto the ground, unable to hold herself up anymore. Her breathing is labored. I wonder if her ribs are broken, too.

"What did the Nephilim do to you?" I whisper.

Zuh grits her teeth. "Doesn't matter. I'll be fine. Just go."

I stand, gripping Smite at my side. Zuh looks intently at me, as though she's imparting me courage, and I nod.

No more words need to be said.

At first, the Nephilim's scent is easy to follow. It's sharp and rancid, and I think Loki might have gone unwashed a little too long. If Nephilim ever wash. It's hard to imagine such vile creatures being concerned about hygiene. But a hundred yards from where I left Zuh, the scent disappears without a trace.

I frown and pause. Should I go back? Ask Zuh what to do? No. She wouldn't want me to. She'd tell me I'm capable of figuring this out myself.

I stand very still and sift through the odors in the air. There are the scents of spring, which are year-round in Antarktos: blooming things, pollen, the threat of rain. I smell animals, things decaying and...

There.

That's a warm scent I recognize.

Aquila!

Here the scent trail takes a sharp turn. It's almost too much to hope, but what if that means Aquila escaped and ran in the other direction? But then where did the Nephilim go?

I push the questions out of my mind and move faster, scrambling down hilly slopes, climbing over rocky ridges. But I've gone too fast. The scent fades out into nothing.

I turn around and head back, but there is no back. It's just me in the unrecognizable jungle, having run too far, too fast, with no idea how to return to Zuh, never mind home. At this realization, my heartbeat goes wild, and I struggle against the feeling of panic.

Aquila needs me, I remind myself.

I backtrack slowly, looking for broken branches and disturbed leaves that I've left in my wake. But I must have disturbed even the air, because nothing smells right. I can't pick up Aquila's scent.

I mentally flagellate myself with every step. Any self-respecting hunter could follow a trail—especially her sister's. And even though my father was *technically* the last hunter, we've been trained in their skillsets in case we ever need them—like now. How I wish my parents were here with me. Or even my older brother, Samuel. He's never been interested in fighting or tracking or any other hunter skills—but he's steady and reliable, and even his presence would give me courage.

A longing for home pierces me, and I feel tears pushing against my eyes. Again. To be at home, with my wise father, my fearless mother, Samuel…and even Aquila, with all her irritating zeal and her overwhelming personality. Her loud ferocity sometimes makes me feel unheard, but I know she loves me. I have to get her back.

I wipe the tears away and look around. It's getting dark. I need to camp out somewhere.

And then I see it—something I'd missed in my rush through the woods earlier: a rocky opening in the hillside.

A cave.

Avoid caves.

Do not enter the underworld.

Ever.

I've heard these lessons all my life, including just a few days ago, when Aquila and I set out with Zuh. But I see little choice, and a solitary cave isn't much threat compared to sleeping out in the open with a Nephilim stalking the woods.

Upon exploration, the cave is the perfect size for me. The opening is small enough to keep cresties and Nephilim out. And if a smaller animal stumbles upon my hideout, I could eat it.

With that thought, my stomach awakens. I haven't eaten all day—and I didn't eat much the day before, either. We were supposed to hunt with Zuh, to practice killing, skinning and cooking an animal. So much for that.

Trying to ignore the hunger, I walk back into the cave. It extends further than I can see, and I don't want to go back there without a light. *What if something lives in there?* What if this is an entrance to the underworld? I shiver and move back toward the opening.

Then I build a fire. I need light—not just to see, but for company. The dark is making me feel lonely.

As soon as I've settled in the cave and lit the tinder, a deluge of rain shakes the rainforest and pools on the ground outside, soaking everything. It's a good thing I gathered the firewood when I did. I stare out at the rain, thinking about the gnawing pain in my stomach and the dryness of my throat. Even a cup of water would do wonders.

That's when I make the connection—it's raining.

I can collect and drink the water provided by the sky itself. I feel stupid for not thinking of it sooner, but I'm outside with the pouch on my belt open before I can dwell on it for long. I drink several pouchfuls until my stomach feels swollen and gurgly.

Back in the cave, the sound of rain threatens to lull me to sleep. I lean against the cool stone wall and stare at the fire, one hand resting on Smite.

I'm half-asleep when I hear a tapping noise. Not like dripping rain. More like...

Feet.

Something is coming out of the depths of the cave.

Something from the underworld.

4

It's faceless. And white. And it has more legs than I can count.

I freeze, mouth agape, as I watch a massive centipede crawl out from the darkness and into the firelight. Its body doesn't seem to have an end. It just keeps coming. What I *can* see is over twenty feet long.

I feel one of the bad words my mom uses rising to the tip of my tongue. "Holy..."

The creature is ten feet away now. I leap to my feet, Smite in my sweaty hand.

The beast tilts its faceless head at me and surges forward, stretching up and reaching for me with its mandibles.

I scream as I swing my hammer toward its front legs. One snaps off, the exoskeleton cracking and dropping a glob of white fat onto the floor. But that doesn't stop the giant centipede's attack. Its mandibles sink into the meat of my shoulder. A deep pain radiates from the bite, skin and muscle tearing, and I scream louder. I fall backward, and the creature's legs flail over my body as it seeks to grab hold. The mandibles release and emerge from my shoulder, covered in blood—my blood. Then it heads for my neck.

I roll out from under the beast, shoulder flowing red, good arm still wielding Smite. Then I run away from its groping, twitching maw and slam my hammer down on its body, ten feet back from the head. The blow is deflected by the solid, almost bonelike carapace. I look further down the cave at its long, undulating body, searching for a weak spot, but I find none.

The centipede's head swoops at me. With a shout, more of surprise than a battle cry, I swing my hammer toward the side of the head. But the centipede moves past me...and around me. In a blur of motion, the creature wraps its body around my legs, squeezing, keeping me from running away. Smite is knocked from my grasp. And then the white head leers at my neck, mandibles hovering, ready to pounce.

"No!" I shriek, hands up, as though telling it to stop.

The centipede snaps to a stop, tilting its head like it didn't expect to be berated by its meal.

"Don't eat me!" I sob. "Let me go!"

The confused centipede loosens its grip on my legs. I wrestle free as the blank insect face lowers toward mine. I snatch Smite off of the floor and, with a legitimate battle cry, I hit the centipede in the head as hard as I can.

The head splits open, and the centipede flops to the ground, dead.

I stand over its body, breathing heavily, heart racing so fast it fills me with nausea. I bend to throw up, but all that comes out of me is water. My whole body shakes from the effort and fear.

I've never seen one of these creatures before, but I have heard of them. The giant subterranean centipedes are an integral part of the underworld's food web. At this size, they're apex predators. But when they're smaller, they're food for a wide assortment of creatures, including hunters. My father credits the creature's fatty insides with keeping him alive on several occasions, both as a food and as an antibiotic that helped heal wounds quickly.

Thinking of food reawakens my hunger.

Stomach growling, I look down at the massive creature.

The creature I killed.

By myself.

Ignoring my hint of a smile, I decide to try cracking it like a nut. I pick up Smite with my good arm and hammer the centipede's body. My blows are ineffective at first, because

I'm still shaky and weak. But after a few solid blows, the exoskeleton shatters, and the white, fatty cream inside the centipede oozes out.

The tangy smell hits me like a counterattack. I take a step back, hand over my nose and mouth, my still-leaking shoulder throbbing from the movement. "Oh..."

You need to eat, I tell myself. *You need your strength.*

So I kneel beside the centipede and scoop its flesh into my hands. It's thick and sludgy, like warm cream cheese. I grimace. "You smell worse than the Nephilim."

I hesitate to lift my hands to my face and eat the goop, but I decide to trust my father's stories. Steeling myself, I take a big bite.

Then I nearly gag.

The texture is slimy and horrible—it tastes like fertilizer—but when I swallow, my stomach practically jumps for joy. So I keep eating.

Once I've stuffed myself with the fatty goo, I look down at my swollen, bloody shoulder. I've got to do something about the wound so it doesn't keep bleeding or get infected. I turn back to the cracked open centipede. Somehow smearing that stuff in an open wound offends me more than consuming it. But again, I decide to trust my father's stories, which I'm starting to realize weren't entirely stories. They were lessons.

Gingerly, I rub the white stuff onto my shoulder. It stings at first, but then it has a cooling effect. I sigh as some of the pain is numbed.

After applying a bandage of torn fabric, I rinse off my bloody arm and my goopy hands in the rain, and then I settle back into my spot by the fire. And for the first time since I set out on this horrible adventure, despite my horrific and now dead companion, I'm able to get some real rest.

As usual, I dream of home, of sleeping in my bed, surrounded by the thick, protective stone room set deep in my family's castle. And then the dream turns dark. It always does. There's someone standing at the foot of the bed, huge black eyes staring at me, wading into my mind and channeling my thoughts. The cold voice intrudes...

You are weak.

Then, a change in the dream I return to night after night, a change in the voice I have become so familiar with: the voice becomes rougher, warmer.

More human.

I'm back in the cave, my slumber ended.

"You couldn't even stay awake." The words contain a dark chuckle.

I frown and sit up, only to find that I'm sitting on a gritty stone floor, the ashes of my fire gray by my feet. A man stands in front of me, a man with a shriveled face, angular muscles under wrinkled skin, flaming eyes...and blood red hair.

A hunter.

Or is it Loki?

I shriek and attempt to scramble to my feet. A thick wooden staff strikes me in the side, knocking me down. My lungs feel squashed, and I gasp for air.

The old man grins at me. "Where is your fight, little girl?"

I force a couple of quick breaths and reach behind me for Smite, where it lies on the ground. But with a flick of his staff, the man knocks it away from me, out of my reach.

I sit up slowly, clutching my side, wheezing. "You're a hunter."

"And you are a princess." The hunter sneers at me, lips thin with age, his red beard wiry and untamed. Then he's squinting, eyeing my face. "I see him in you, your grandfather. How disappointed he would be."

"How did you find me?"

The hunter gestures to the pile of ash on the floor. "You built a fire, foolish one. You practically signaled me."

I curse in my mind. How did I not think of that? Looking at his blood-red hair, I remember what the color speaks of: corruption. Slavery to the Nephilim. "You don't need to serve them anymore," I say. "The Nephilim. The hunters were freed."

"Not all hunters wanted your father's kind of freedom," he says with disgust.

"You didn't want a new life?"

His eyes glint with fury. "I will die for my master before I submit to your king."

"Who is your master?" I lean toward Smite, keeping my eyes fixed on him, taunting him.

"I serve Freya, Goddess of Life, soon to be Goddess of All of Antarktos." His eyes grow wide, crazed. "You could no more stop the masters than you could the relentless winds of Antarktos."

My hand is almost at Smite's handle now. "Your goddess will never rule Antarktos," I say. "My father controls even the winds of Antarktos. The Nephilim have been defeated forever."

Those words send him over the edge, just as I intended. He lunges at me, incensed. I lurch the last few inches to Smite and duck his blow. His staff strikes the ground, the clatter ringing throughout the cavern.

Then I step to my feet and swing, striking one of the hunter's hands.

It cracks loudly, bones shattering.

He screams and whips the staff at my feet, but I jump over it just in time. While he's turning from momentum, I swing again, but miss. He regains control of his staff and thrusts the end into my stomach, pushing me back and knocking the air out of me again. I double over, incapacitated as I struggle to breathe.

He moves toward me and twirls the staff in his good hand. Before, he was using the blunt end. Now I see a blade.

"You could walk out of this cave," I say, all taunting gone. "You could walk out of this cave and be free. Forgiven. Even loved."

He snarls. "Never!"

I strike the side of his staff with Smite. It doesn't fall from his hands, but it's enough of a distraction for me to run. Back into the cave, back where the light doesn't reach.

His feet pound after me, but he's a lot older than me, and my legs are faster. Better than that—I'm smaller. I run with one hand against the cavern wall to guide me. After a couple of hundred yards, the wall drops out from beneath my hand. I reach back and discover a crevice—just big enough for me to squirm inside. I pull myself up into the nook and twist myself into its bowels, following the path that probably brought the centipede into the cave. A path that I'm sure leads into the underworld.

Confident I'm out of reach, I stop to breathe. My lungs burn, pressing against my aching sides and stomach. I'm definitely going to have a bruise—more than one.

The hunter's footsteps get closer and closer...and stop. I hold my breath, which is painful because my lungs are screaming for air.

"I know you're there." His rough voice crawls through the rock and makes me shiver. He's going to catch me. He's going to crawl back here, and I'll be trapped.

Then I realize.

Despite being lanky and thin, he's too big to fit in the crevice. I could cry from relief.

The anger in his voice is barely contained. "The way forward leads to a realm you cannot survive. Come back, and I will spare your life. If you continue forward, I will find you, little girl, and I will kill you."

My answer is to start squirming deeper.

5

The tunnel widens, and before long I don't have to crouch to navigate. I do, however, have to walk carefully, because the tunnel slopes steeply downward. I'm descending into the place my parents told me never to go.

The realization freaks me out. I am not a fan of the under-world—after all, the remaining Nephilim live down here. Maybe. And apparently some hunters, too. And thirty-foot-long centipedes. I shudder at the thought. But I can't go back. That hunter knows I was there, and if he's lying in wait… I'd be dead before I could count to three.

So I move onward.

Until I slip.

Loose gravel under my feet sends me sprawling. I slide down the steep grade, unable to get a handhold or to stop myself. As the tunnel curves downward, becoming a chute, I accelerate. It shuttles me down and deposits me hard on a rock floor. Pain shoots up from my tail bone, following the course of my spine and radiating out through my ribs as my core compresses.

Sitting in the darkness, I groan. Everything aches. I don't want to get up or move or keep trying to find Aquila. My shoulder hurts, my side hurts, my stomach hurts, and now pretty much everything else hurts from hitting the ground. After a minute, I stand and stretch, popping things back into place. Then I step out of the corner where I was dropped into a clearing.

A clearing that I can see. There's dim light here, as though the underground vault is glowing. More than that—the walls are speckled with light. I run my hands along the surface and find that the lights are sharp and hard, like crystals. I pull a loose one out of the wall. It is, in fact, a crystal, and it's glowing. Have I heard about these, too? I think so, but I suspect my parents excluded anything about the underworld that might fascinate a child. The stories I heard most were about hard-ship, death and woe.

I move the crystal around, illuminating the area near me. *A makeshift flashlight,* I decide. I'm going to need it. I can't face the world down here if I can't see it.

I see a path leading out of the clearing, and I take it. It leads downward, but at a more gradual angle. Now that I can see the ground, I'm able to keep my footing. This tunnel links up with a wider tunnel—one that has been traveled recently. The rocks scattering the ground have been disturbed, and a faint scent hangs in the air. I bend to the ground and sniff. It's a scent I recognize.

Aquila!

I breathe deeply, and the smell brings a wave of emotion. Memories of playing 'Hunter' in the castle garden, battling each other, pretending that we were fighting the Nephilim. Memories of before I was afraid, back when Aquila and I bonded over a passion for the fight and our naïve courage.

She was here. The Nephilim took her underground. But which direction do I go?

I look up and down the tunnel. To the right, the tunnel slopes downward, and the rocks seem to have scattered in that direction. Of course they would have brought her deeper, farther from the surface, farther from salvation. But to follow her...that means I have to go deeper, too. Deeper than I ever wanted to go, and farther from everything I know.

I stand from my crouching position and rest my hand on Smite. Then I set out, deeper into the darkness.

I lose count of the hours. Life underground is one long, endless night. It's quieter than nighttime in the forest, although my footfalls echo ominously along the walls. I move as quickly and as quietly as I can, because I'm sure the hunter is still looking for me, tracking me, staff prepared to strike me down.

And then there is sound. It starts as a faint whooshing that grows into the pounding rush of water. An underground river—one of many I've been told flow through subterranean Antarktos. Life-giving veins of water. The thought of quenching my thirst pushes me on, and my stealthy movement turns into a careless run. Perhaps there will be animals near the water—any kind of creature, as long as I can eat it.

The tunnel widens into a huge arch, leading to a wide cavern, carved out by centuries of moving water. But I hardly notice. I kneel at the shoreline and dunk my whole face in the river, drinking mouthfuls at a time. It is cold and clean and purifying. Reinvigorated, I feel like I could walk another ten miles.

A loud noise—something between a honk and a moan—startles me. I lift my head, wipe the water out of my eyes, and see it. A cresty, one giant claw pinning a dead animal—probably its lunch—to the ground, his head craned toward me. Watching. While most cresties moved to the surface when the continent thawed, there are some who remained below ground, too well adapted to living in the dark to ever set foot in the light again. Like some hunters, I suppose.

I sit very still, hoping he decides I'm a part of the landscape, hoping he'll turn away. But he doesn't. Lunch forgotten, he takes a step toward me.

I reach toward my hammer. I don't know if the cresties underground are friendly to uncorrupted humans, like most of those topside, but I doubt they know we are allies.

The creature bellows again.

"Good cresty," I whisper.

I swear he squints at me.

I clutch Smite, and in the second the cresty sees me going for my weapon, he tenses. All the muscles in his back ripple under his tough skin. He steps forward again, guarding his lunch.

I can feel my heartbeat racing in my chest. But I focus on the weight of the hammer in my hand. I've already killed a thirty-foot centipede and escaped a hunter. I have gained some skills on this training trip—more than I wanted. But I will need them now...or I will get eaten by a dinosaur.

I think about the cresties aboveground. Whenever our family traveled, Aquila and I rode on their backs, our parents seated in front of us. Because the cresties were so big, they lumbered slowly. But when angry, they knew how to attack—to reach out with their long necks and serrated teeth, tearing apart anything that got in their way.

This guy's about fifteen feet tall. Not fully grown, so he won't be as heavy and slow as the older dinosaurs. But I hope that also means he's not as smart.

A story comes to my mind. My mother once faced off against a large cresty. The creature was named Alice by my father, who has a penchant of naming creatures based on fictional characters from his childhood. Alice was a thirty-foot-long matriarch, and my mother fought the creature with her hammer. And lost. This cresty is half the size of Alice, but I'm also half the size of my mother, and I'm a far less capable fighter. If not for my father rescuing her, my mother would have been eaten.

So my fate seems fairly well sealed.

Unless I can do better than my mother.

Not better, or stronger, I think. *Different.*

There's a pile of rocks by my feet. With a sideways kick, I dislodge them and send them clattering and splashing into the river. The cresty turns his head for a moment.

And that's when I strike.

I jump forward, running as fast as I can for the cresty's side. He swings his long neck around, and I aim my hammer's strike at his head.

He swings up and out of the way at the last second. Okay, this guy is smart. Probably hardened by his years underground. But I'm still spinning, hammer in the air. With a battle cry, I take my momentum and charge at his leg.

I land a solid blow.

The cresty cries out in anger and pain. I look up at his gleaming teeth and lose focus. In that second, something heavy collides with my legs and knocks my feet out from under me. As I fall, I see his thick tail finish its swing.

Splayed on the ground, staring up at the jagged ceiling, I struggle to regain my breath. My back screams in pain from the impact. The cavern looks like it's rotating as it fades in and out of my vision.

And then the cresty's head appears above me. He leans over me, staring with some mixture of curiosity and frustration. Then he lets out a low moan that reminds me of a growl.

"Good cresty...good cresty," I say again. I feel for my hammer. But it's not in my hand or by my side. I turn my head and see it twenty feet away on the stone floor. I must have let go of it when he struck me. So much for outdoing my mother.

Fear rises up in my chest, a behemoth inside me, but I fight it. I am a hunter. Hunters do not show fear. Hunters die honorable deaths. And that's what I'm determined to do, as I stare up into the face of the pissed-off cresty. I meet his eyes and stare at him with all the courage and defiance I can muster.

6

The cresty stares back. The muscles around his eyes relax, and he looks at me with a strange softness.

"What?" I ask. "Are you not hungry?"

He tilts his head and gives a low grumble.

I decide to take my chances and stand up. As I move, he pulls his head back and lowers it, as though bowing to me. The only time I've ever seen this kind of subservience in a cresty is when one approaches my father. It's how they defer to their leader, their king.

I frown. Does this cresty somehow know that I am daughter to the King of Antarktos? But then, why did it fight me in the first place? I'll have to test my theory.

Stepping slowly, eyes on my adversary, I retrieve Smite and then move over to the heap of animal remains that was the cresty's lunch. I don't know what animal it was—it's been mauled beyond recognition—but I decide to take my chances. "I'm hungry," I declare, and I draw a knife out of my pouch, carving a slice of raw flesh off of the animal.

The cresty does not attack in anger over me taking its meal. Instead, it stays a few steps away, head bowed.

I *am* actually hungry, so I eat the flesh I've taken. It's slippery and clearly uncooked, but it's much tastier than centipede slop. The first bite awakens the hunger I've been ignoring, and I dig into the animal, eating as quickly as I can. But then I feel guilty. Not only did I beat up this poor cresty, but I've taken its meal.

I stare at it for a moment, and then look up and down the tunnel, embarrassed by what I'm considering. Seeing no one and nothing—thank God—I turn back to the cresty.

"Come," I say through a mouthful of hearty flesh, waving with one arm.

It feels ridiculous and stupid. Although cresties are trainable—they're smarter than dogs—wild cresties are known to be unpredictable and unruly.

The cresty blinks, and then lumbers to my side and waits.

I watch it, mouth agape. It takes a few moments for my shock to wear off and my jaws to snap shut. Then I say, "Eat."

My eyebrows rise in time with the creature's lowering head. And then it joins me in my feast.

This is beyond strange. The cresty follows my commands. It should have been angry enough to kill me. And it has no way of knowing that my father is the King—unless there's some sort of supernatural power at work.

Supernatural power.

I pause, bloody knife in hand, fingers still covered in the meat's juices, as I ponder this idea. Father has supernatural powers. He controls Antarktos itself. He's connected to it, and has been since the day of his birth, when the 'whole continent groaned'—at least, according to his tale. He can move any part of the land, water, or air, and he can feel disturbances to those elements. And as far as I know, nobody else has powers like his...

Except, maybe, his children?

My mind whirls at the possibility.

Perhaps I, too, have powers like my father's. I was born on Antarktos. I am an Antarktican, the daughter of the Last Hunter, who was himself the very first Antarktican. It was for those reasons that my dad had powers—that, and he was pretty much the chosen one for the Nephilim. The story of my birth tickles my memory, but doesn't fully resolve. I haven't heard it in many years. And as far as I know, the Nephilim have no interest in me.

But maybe...

I concentrate, thinking of the water in the air, thinking of rain. Maybe I can create a raindrop. Maybe...

I open my eyes.

Not a speck of wetness—not on my skin, not on the ground. I sigh.

The cresty watches me.

I flush, embarrassed. "What are you looking at?"

He looks away, head hung in shame.

It's as if he understands me. Weird. I sigh and stand up, looking at my hands. They're crusted with animal blood and other meat juices. gross.

"I'm going to rinse off," I say, half for the cresty's sake and half for my own. Maybe so I don't feel like I'm losing my mind.

I walk down to the river's shore and step in, bending down to let the water flow over my hands. Its cool touch soothes me, washing away my tension. I can't believe I've come this far—I'm underground, pursuing the Nephilim, being chased by a hunter. The idea would have terrified the Norah I knew yesterday. And it still terrifies me a little—but I also feel invigorated. I've fought better than I thought I could, and I've found strength I didn't know I had. And I've survived. I've found food and water, as well as built two fires on my own.

This is why my parents and Zuh wanted me to train. Maybe they were right all along, when they told me these skills were necessary. I never believed them. The Antarktos I've always known is such a peaceful place. After the Earth's crustal shift, many survivors migrated here, where the climate is warm and tropical. Many people who hadn't died in the chaos had been displaced by drastic changes in temp-erature—raging heat in some places, freezing cold and snow in others. So Antarktos became a home, and not just to my family. People from different cultures came together to create a utopia of sorts. We had to work together to defeat the Nephilim and take back the continent. And my father is a good ruler—kind, just, brave. Because of that, Antarktos is the safest it's ever been. And I had not wanted to believe that a much darker world lay beneath the surface. A world where some Nephilim still survive and where hunters carry out their wishes.

But here, in the river, it's almost peaceful. The water is cleansing. Pure.

I take off my belt and leave it by the bank, so that my sketchpad doesn't get wet. And then I wade further in.

The river is wide and shallow on the edges, so I have to walk a good twenty yards before the water hits my belly button. Here, the water is choppier. I let the rush of the river envelop me, and I dive.

As soon as my feet aren't touching the bottom, the current drags me down, and I know I've made a mistake. I writhe against its pull, but I can't return to the surface. I can't touch the bottom either. The river spins my body, pulling me head over heels and leaving me disoriented. My lungs burn. On the inside, I'm screaming, *Help!* But on the outside, I can't say a thing.

My head strikes something—the river bottom? I open my mouth to cry out in pain, and water fills my throat. I see blood in the water, swirling past me as the current yanks me downriver. Then I see something else—something big and dark moving toward me.

I wave my arms like a panicking turkuin, trying to escape, but the blood trail is a dead giveaway. The river has given its sentence. I close my eyes as the oxygen runs out and the water tingles in my lungs.

7

Death is colder than I expected. And wet. Then I'm coughing. I'm coughing up water and sucking in air as fast as I possibly can. Not dead. My head throbs. I wipe the stinging water out of my eyes and realize I'm dangling over the river, suspended in something's grasp. Something that is pulling at the back of my leather shirt.

I twist my head back as far as I can, and I see the cresty lumbering through the water, holding my clothes gently in its jaws. He saved me. The cresty *saved me*.

He sets me down on the riverbank and climbs out of the water to stand beside me.

"Thank you," I say, voice raspy from coughing.

He nudges me with his head, as if to make sure I'm okay.

"I'm alright, thanks to you." I stand up, shivering. That was too close to death for my liking. And now I'm cold. The damp rock walls offer no warmth or comfort.

The cresty moves closer and nudges for me to sit. I obey, and he settles next to me, offering his warm, broad back for me to lean on. When I do, he curls his tail around me. I'm the warmest I've been since I came underground.

"How did you know?" I ask, knowing he can't answer. "How did you know I was drowning? Why did you save me?"

As expected, the cresty doesn't respond. I'm sure he can't understand what I'm saying. And yet...he came for me. He bowed to me, let me eat his food and then came to save my life, even when I couldn't call for help.

Or did I?

In my mind, I was screaming for help. Maybe...maybe I called him, somehow, through my mind and my will. And maybe he obeyed me. What if I have the power to control this cresty?

Maybe even more than just the cresty?

I close my eyes and think hard about the belt that I left on the riverbank, willing the cresty to get up and retrieve it for me.

When the cresty moves, taking away my makeshift back-rest, I almost topple over. He's standing, moving down the shore toward my belt. He's obeying me! I'm controlling a dinosaur!

He brings the belt back to me, the strap held loosely in his mouth, and sets it on the ground.

"Thank you." I smile at the cresty, as I fasten the belt around my waist. He looks so magnificent standing there, bold, thick stripes on his textured skin, his crested head held high on his solid tree trunk of a neck. "Wait. Stay there." I hold up one hand and dig through the pouch on my belt, drawing out my sketchpad and charcoals.

As I flip through old sketches, searching for a blank page, I see my half-finished drawing of the agouti—the little creature who had posed for me in the woods when I was escaping Aquila and Zuh.

Aquila.

The memory brings a sudden surge of guilt. How could I have let myself get so distracted? I'm on a mission. I have to save her.

But something about the drawing of the agouti makes me pause. I stare at him and realize it's his eyes. It's like he's making eye contact with me from the page—just as he was when I met him in the forest. Most little animals like that don't meet a human's eyes with such fearlessness.

That's when I realize.

The agouti wasn't afraid of me. The agouti was drawn to me. In fact...*I* might have drawn him to me. Somehow,

I communicated with this creature, and he sat still so I could sketch him—just like the cresty is doing now.

Just like the centipede in the cave. I told it to let me go, and it did.

That's when the story of my birth resolves from the far reaches of my memory. It wasn't my parents who told me—it was Aunt Mira, crouched next to my bed, her crazy blonde hair tickling my cheek. She was there. At my birth. She caught me. "Just as my mother was there to catch your father," she had said. "My father told me that when Solomon was born, all of Antarctica—the *whole* continent—groaned at his birth. But with you, it wasn't the continent, it was the animals. From the largest to the smallest. The moment your small body reached my hands, they cried out to welcome you."

I always thought she was just telling stories to put me to sleep. I never dreamed she was telling the truth.

My heart sinks as I realize that's the only reason I survived my fight with the centipede. Without this power, I'd be dead a couple of times over. My skills as a hunter didn't save me. My powers as an Antarktican did.

Maybe I'm not as good of a hunter as I thought.

I suddenly feel faint. My head pounds, reminding me of its bump against the river bottom. I touch my hand to the area, and it comes away stained red. I groan inwardly. Another head wound.

For the first time in the last several minutes, the cresty moves. He raises his head, alert, muscles tense.

I tense, too. And I listen. Sniff. I look past the cresty, down into the cave.

There's nothing to be seen, but I can smell him.

The hunter.

I think a direct thought, aimed at the cresty.

We need to go.

The cresty crouches down, and I jump onto his back. Seated firmly with Smite at my side, I urge him forward, down into the river. The water hinders our speed some, but we're able to move without leaving a trail.

I look behind us and see a flash of red hair.

The movement makes me dizzy. I look down and see that the blood is dripping down my shoulder and arm. I have to remind myself that it's mixed with water, which makes it look much worse than it is. I'm okay. I'm still conscious. At least, that's what I'm telling myself. But with every heavy step as the cresty moves through the water, my head pulses with pain.

I must have communicated this to the cresty, because he stops.

No. Keep moving, I think.

He moves, but more slowly. Even his gentle lumbering walk makes my head scream with pain. Everything starts to spin.

I loosen my belt and strap myself to the cresty's neck. I don't think I'm going to stay conscious much longer...

So I give one last command.

Don't let the hunter get us.

8

I wake up in darkness.

I move to sit up, but the pulsing pain in my head keeps me down. So I wait for my eyes to adjust to the light, and then I have a look around.

I'm in an alcove of sorts—only about four or five feet in every direction. To my left is an opening, just three feet wide, where a faint light seeps through, as though the entrance is blocked by something.

How did I get here?

I touch my head and find a crusty scab about an inch and a half long. The skin around it is tender and hot, but at least the bleeding has stopped. I roll onto my stomach, holding my breath against the pain pounding through my skull. Then I scoot toward the opening and touch whatever's blocking it.

It's warm.

And it moves.

My heart races as the blockade pulls away from the opening—and then I see the cresty's face, lowered to greet me.

"Hey," I say, almost laughing. "You startled me." I crawl out of the alcove and sit next to the cresty. My belt hangs loosely around his neck, and I untie it, wrapping it around my waist again. "You're a good boy." I stroke his head, feeling overwhelmingly thankful. Somehow we escaped the hunter. And somehow, this dinosaur found a way to hide me.

"You need a name," I say, as I pet him. I think he might be purring. He has been a good friend to me—has saved my life more than once already and led me out of danger. I think of another man who led his friends out of danger, a man in the Bible stories my Dad reads us before we go to sleep at night. "How about Moses?"

The cresty makes a happy noise, and I laugh for real this time. "Moses it is."

We're still by the river, but we must be much farther downstream. The air feels colder here, as though we're deeper underground. My gut wrenches. How many hundreds of feet below home am I? Will I be trapped in this burial ground forever?

Aquila will be, if I don't figure out a way to save her. I have to make a plan, figure out where I'm going and still keep this hunter off my tail. I'm sure we've only delayed him by hiding downriver. And with this bloody mass on my head—which is probably infected—my scent is going to be much easier to find.

A centipede would be useful right about now, I think. He'd not only feed us, but his flesh would help heal my wounds and disguise our scent. Too bad I haven't seen any more on my journey so far.

I turn to Moses, my mouth open in my newfound revelation. "I can call one!"

He just stares at me, with fond, blank eyes.

I close my eyes and focus, envisioning a centipede crawling toward us along the bank, calling, *Come.*

And then I look along the shore, along the walls, hoping to see one scuttling out of a crevice. But I don't see a single centipede. My shoulders sag in disappointment. I shoot a pouty face at Moses, and I glimpse something over his shoulder...something big and greenish-white, something crawling up out of the water. A centipede shakes the river water off its legs and moves toward us.

"I didn't know they were amphibious," I whisper.

Moses smells the creature and turns to look. Once he sees the centipede, he makes an angry noise—probably the closest thing a dinosaur can get to an irritated whinny. He steps forward as if to attack.

"No," I say. "Let me get this one."

I draw the centipede toward me. Its antennae flick about, confused. It is powerless against me.

But I have to prove something to myself. And so I drop all control over the creature.

Suddenly awake to its own will, the centipede rears its head. This one is even larger than the one in the cave. It must be fifty feet long. Perhaps amphibious centipedes have a better chance at survival than the ones on land? With longevity comes size. I didn't even know such things existed, and I don't think my father did either.

It lurches toward me, furious, antennae twitching. But I have my hammer at the ready. With a glancing blow, I hit it in the center of the forehead.

It sways backward, disoriented. But I haven't cracked the carapace. Time to try again. It settles its front feet on the ground and scuttles toward me, walking around me and trapping me in a ten-foot circle with its body.

Moses grunts again, but I hold up a hand, telling him to stay. He waits impatiently.

I grip Smite and prepare to strike again, harder this time. The last blow was not forceful enough. One clean strike should break open the head. But this amphibious creature seems to have a tougher shell than its land-based cousins.

The centipede swings its face toward me again, and this time its eyes meet mine. The first centipede I met did not have eyes like this. They are big, glossy and dark against its white features. They're like black holes staring into my soul.

My lungs clench and I feel like I can't breathe. In the back of my mind I see the soulless eyes again, hear the taunting voice: *You are weak.*

Just like that, I'm no longer present in my surroundings. I'm in my room as it was a year ago, unfortified, alone. Until the Nephilim walks in and seeps into my mind, holding me captive in a prison of myself.

I never slept in that room again.

A loud noise brings me back to the underworld. Moses has stepped on the centipede right behind its head, pinning it down as it squirms. He looks at me as though asking for permission.

I shake my head and walk three steps to stand over the creature, looking down into its empty eyes. Arms shaking, I pick up Smite and hammer its head until it cracks. The centipede stills, and Moses steps back.

I'm breathing heavily, and sweat streams down my brow. When I reach up to wipe it away, my forehead nearly burns to the touch. It's time for centipede ointment.

Break it open, I command, and Moses stomps on the shell. White flesh oozes out, and I bathe my head in it, smearing globs into my dark blonde hair, and then again on my shoulder.

"That should do the trick," I say.

And that's when I see it: an army of centipedes crawling up out of the river.

9

"Oh..." I look over at Moses, whose eyes are wide. He bellows, but I can't tell if it's out of anger or fear.

I guess I must have summoned *all* the nearby centipedes. There are at least fifty. Some are the size of my arm. Others are monsters, like the one lying dead in front of me. My stomach turns. These creatures were all around us, and I had no idea. They could have attacked while I was sleeping, and I wouldn't have been able to stop all of them.

But—where were they living? The river here is slower, but the moving water would prevent them from building any sort of nest...right? Unless there's a pond nearby. Which means that maybe the downhill slope flattens out up ahead...

I shake my head. I have to forget about our geographic location for the moment. The mass of centipedes is still swarming toward us.

I close my eyes and focus. Then I imagine all of the centipedes slowing down and stopping, waiting patiently for further commands.

When I open my eyes, they have slowed down, but they haven't stopped. I guess my command wasn't strong enough. So I think the word this time: *Stop.*

About half of the centipedes slow tentatively to a halt, as if they're not really sure what they're doing. The rest continue oozing forward.

Maybe it takes more energy to stop a group this size. I inhale deeply, fighting nausea and an aching exhaustion in my skull. Then I hold my hands out in a gesture that clearly says, *Don't come any closer.* And with every bit of energy I have, as though I'm pushing against the force of the fifty huge amphibious creatures in front of me, I will the centipedes to stop.

And they do.

I breathe a sigh of relief and lower my hands to my sides, but keep my mental guard up, unsure if they will stop following my commands as soon as I relax.

Moses growls.

I turn to him, confused—after all, haven't I just neutralized the enemy? But I realize he's no longer looking at the centipedes. He's looking behind me.

I whirl around, whipping Smite off my belt and holding it at the ready. And I see what Moses saw. The hunter who has been pursuing me—and four other hunters standing at his side. I size them up. The four new hunters are relatively big and muscular, but like the hunter I recognize, their skin is wrinkled and their faces look almost shriveled. One of the hunters even has a bit of a hunchback. They all have wiry red hair—red hair that I suppose would be gray, if it wasn't corrupted by Nephilim influence.

"Looks like you've got a bit of a centipede infestation," the first hunter sneers. "Need some help?"

"I thought hunters didn't work together," I say, infusing contempt into my voice. I will *not* sound afraid. Not in front of my enemies, and not with a small army at my command.

"Old friends," my hunter sneers.

"Old, for sure." I laugh, mocking. "You all look like you're due to die soon."

The hunchbacked hunter lurches forward at this, but my hunter stays him with a hand. "You don't have very good manners for a princess," he says. The word *princess* is clearly intended as an insult.

"I'm a hunter," I say through gritted teeth. It's only after the words come out of my mouth that I realize how much I'm starting to sound like Aquila. The memory of my sister makes me grip my hammer tighter, and I feel my eyes light with a new fury.

My hunter laughs. "You are no hunter. You are a frightened little girl."

"Where is my sister?"

He laughs again. "Oh, you don't need to worry. Freya is taking very good care of her."

Freya.

The goddess he serves. Despite my best efforts, my stomach twists in fear. "Who is Freya, and where can I find her?"

He smiles at me. "Freya is the one who wants you dead."

I can't control my anger anymore, anger that is gaining new strength from my fear. A surge of willpower flows through my body, and I thrust my hands forward, commanding the centipedes to advance.

I hear the huge, scuttling rush behind me. And then they're swarming around me, headed straight for the hunters.

My hunter's eyes widen in awe. He knows I command this army now. I will not let him use that knowledge against me.

With his staff, he whips away the first few centipedes, bashing in the heads of some. His friends draw out an assortment of knives, whips, throwing stars and chains. But the centipedes are too numerous for them to hold off.

"Men, into the water!" he yells.

I can barely contain a smile when I realize that I know something he doesn't: these centipedes can swim.

The other four hunters dash for the water, centipedes at their heels. My hunter moves closer to me, battling centipedes at every step.

"Who are you?" I yell. "What do you want?"

"Hannibal," he says, spearing a large centipede in the face, while glaring back at me, his confidence unwavering despite the odds. But is he really that confident, or is he, like a good hunter, hiding his emotions? "And *you* need to come with me."

A scream bellows from the river as the hunters realize the centipedes have followed them into the water. They thrash their weapons about, and I send the centipedes deeper, striking at the hunters' feet. Hannibal turns toward the scream, and his thick, untamed red eyebrows raise in horror. He looks at me with a new sort of respect.

He must think I've given the centipedes the power to swim. I keep my hands in the air to heighten this effect. But I don't have to control the centipedes in the water anymore. They're hungry and violent without my help.

"Freya may want this one alive," he mutters. Without taking his eyes off me, he slashes his staff down at a centipede that has approached his feet. It curls on its side, dead.

One of the hunters in the water has fallen—the hunch-backed one, I guess, since that's who's missing—and the centipedes begin fighting over his body. The other hunters take advantage of the distraction and swim across the river, pulling themselves to shore on the other side.

This time, I see Hannibal's staff before it connects. Smite stops the staff with a metallic clang. I will not be swept off my feet again.

I need a moment to focus and summon the remaining centipedes to my side, but Hannibal doesn't give me a break. He strikes and I deflect, over and over. My arms are getting tired and my head throbs. I back up, down the shore toward the river. He moves forward, keeping my pace.

The water laps at my ankles as I step into the river.

With the raging water at my back, I am out of room to flee. The hunter's grin says he understands that, too.

But my grin in return wipes his away.

"Hannibal," I say. "Meet Moses."

The hunter's eyes rise slowly to the sound of a guttural growl. The cresty, who was never far behind, stretches out his neck and chomps at Hannibal's shoulder. Hannibal howls and turns, thrusting his staff at Moses's neck. Moses staggers backward, then grabs the staff in his teeth and rips it away from Hannibal.

While they fight, I thrust my hands forward and command the centipedes out of the water and in Hannibal's direction. They scuttle out of the water and wrap around his ankles, wrestling him to the ground.

He flails without his weapon, as the centipedes reach toward him with their mandibles.

Suddenly I realize what I am doing. I am about to kill him. The centipedes obey me. They are my weapon. And I have given this man a death sentence.

With all of my willpower, I scream, "Stop!"

But it's too late.

The centipedes look up at me, bewildered. Below them lies a mangled man, whose hair I can no longer distinguish from his blood.

Something inside of me collapses. I slump to the ground, all control over the centipedes falling with me. They feast, and I weep.

INTERLUDE 2 OF 2

When Aquila awakened, she couldn't see anything. She closed her eyes and opened them again. Nothing. Except... some pinpricks of light. *Stars? No.* This was darker than the forest at night.

She sat up and rubbed her head. Everything hurt. The air was damp and cold, and the ground unforgiving. It felt like stone.

She swallowed as she remembered the last thing she had seen. Loki's hand swinging toward her. Zuh lying on the ground, bloodied. Probably dead.

Something inside her froze with the realization. Her teacher, her guardian, her friend—dead. All because she hadn't been strong enough or smart enough or fast enough to defeat Loki.

She couldn't cry because she was furious. Furious with herself, and furious with the monster who did this. She would escape. She would make him pay. And if she died from the effort, well, that was what she deserved.

Aquila stood on her sore legs and stretched her hands out, groping through the darkness. She walked forward slowly, so she wouldn't trip on any invisible obstacles. But it took only a few steps for her to find a wall. *Stone floor, stone walls*, she decided. The pinpricks of light she had seen before were buried in the stone— the crystals of the underworld. She recognized them. She and Zuh had spent hours underground. Of course, she had always run ahead, and Zuh had chased after her, reminding her to watch where she was going.

For the first time, Aquila wished she had listened.

Of course, Norah used to run ahead in the jungle, too, until what was probably a nightmare. Norah claimed to have seen a presence in her room, looming, large and taunting, but if a Nephilim had been in her bedroom, *inside* the fortress, her father would have certainly sensed it. Not wanting to cause her parents undue stress because of a bad dream—they were already trying to run a continent and oversee the relocation of millions of refugees—Norah had told only their gentle older brother Samuel. When Aquila had been frustrated at the change in Norah's temperament, Samuel had explained it to her. He made Aquila promise not to say a word. Aquila hoped Norah was okay. If Zuh was dead, Norah was on her own. Maybe she'd gone home to get help. Or maybe Loki had found her, too.

As Aquila thought, she followed the wall with her hands. It curved around and brought her back to where she'd started. From that, she was able to deduce a few things. She was trapped in a pit...in the underworld, which she knew held dire implications. The pit was about twenty feet wide. How high, she didn't know. It was quite empty—strangely empty, she realized, as she thought back on her father's stories. If it *was* a feeder pit, like the one he'd been trapped in so many years ago, it should have feeders in it—or at least feeder bones. But the ground was clean.

Feeder pits were for breaking people—body, mind and soul—so they could be reformed in the Nephilim's image. As hunters. The red-haired, corrupted variety. If she had been put in a feeder pit, that meant they were trying to break her—to steal her memories, and turn her into a mindless, emotionless, soulless hunter they could control. It was worse than that even. If she broke, she would *want* to help the Nephilim. Would serve them gladly. Very few people could break free of the corruption on their own. Even her father had had help, from Aunt Mira's mother.

But if this wasn't a feeder pit—where was she?

And how would she escape?

She began scraping at the wall with her fingernails, trying to free a protruding crystal. If she could pull it out of the wall, she'd have a light source. Until then, she had no tools, no—

Shocked, she reached for her belt, searching for Strike. But the sword was nowhere to be found. All of the tools in her pouch were gone. No flint and steel, no dried jerky, no compass, no nothing.

Whoever put her here did not want her to escape.

But wasn't that the test? Wasn't she supposed to prove herself strong enough by finding a way out, no matter how gruesome or violent the means?

She doubled her efforts, tugging at the partially exposed crystal.

Something above her rumbled. The pit quivered, and the crystal gave way, popping free into her hands. Aquila stood very still. The rumble sounded like...laughter.

If she listened very closely, she thought she could hear air moving above her. Someone breathing. Long breath in. Long breath out. Someone *big*.

A Nephilim.

She ground her teeth together. A Nephilim who would soon taste her sword—as soon as she could get it back. A Nephilim who would face her fury.

"I'm coming for you," she hissed. The whisper echoed in the empty pit.

Gripping the crystal in her teeth, she searched for handholds in the wall. There weren't many, but some of the exposed crystals offered enough grip for her to hold. She scaled eight feet up before she got stuck.

Then the laughter hit again, and the shaking walls sent her falling back to the cavern floor.

A sucking noise drew her attention. She looked up to see a teardrop-shaped sac gleaming in the light, thirty feet overhead, oozing toward the ground.

This *was* a feeder pit, she knew now. But whatever happened, she would *not* be broken.

The sac collapsed and the creature fell with a heavy splat. She frowned. This looked bigger than the feeders she'd heard of. Heavier. The sac should have dropped gently to the ground before the creature emerged, giving her a chance to slay it before it even breathed.

Instead, a five-foot-tall creature—as tall as she was—unraveled itself from its slick bonds and stood to its full height. Its limbs were awkward, long and thin, covered with sprouts of red hair. Its belly hung and swayed over its skinny old man legs. It almost looked like a man, she realized, although its torso was disproportionately short and fat compared to the rest of it. Its broad mouth hung open, drooling and breathing heavily. Twin rows of shark-like teeth filled the maw, no doubt powerful enough to sever her limbs in one quick snap. And the wet, black eyes, nearly popping out of its domed, hairless head... They stared at her, somehow both lifeless and hungry.

Aquila reached for Strike, but it wasn't there. Not for the first time that day, she cursed the Nephilim for their cruelty. But she had learned resourcefulness from Zuh. She had also learned that you could kill a living creature with almost anything. This was no different. She took the crystal out of her mouth and held it like a dagger.

The creature grunted and swayed. Its top-heavy body made its walk an uncomfortable stagger, as though its legs were not quite strong enough to hold the creature up.

She knew climbing up the wall wouldn't help. Even if she could climb out of the creature's reach, she'd fall as soon as the rolling laughter hit. So instead, she circled the creature, giving it her most threatening glare.

It lurched toward her, arms outstretched. She dodged away and kept moving. Every few seconds, it would stagger toward her again. Evading its arms was easy. It had no strategy and no plan, she was sure of that. So all she needed to do was make it tired.

She started running, making her circles smaller and smaller, faster and faster. The creature, no longer able to keep up, flung its head from side to side, watching her. When its arms couldn't keep up and hung limp at its sides, Aquila closed in. She thrust the crystal up into its open mouth and deep into its throat.

The creature gagged. Its eyes went wide and then flat, as it fell to the ground.

Aquila caught her breath and wiped the sweat off her forehead. For a moment, she felt pity for the creature, its naïveté written all over its face. But then her hunger took over. Every survival lesson she'd heard over the years included one unifying theme: eat. Whenever possible, fill your gut. Keep your energy up. Because there is no way to know when your next meal will come. She looked down at the slain creature, sneering with disgust at the idea of consuming it. But she already felt weak, and the fight had tired her more. *If I'm going to survive,* she thought, *and kill these Nephilim, then I need to eat.* After retrieving the bloodied crystal from the creature's throat, she fell to her knees. Using the crystal's jagged edge, she sliced into the monster's thigh.

And she ate.

Three bites.

And then the next monster arrived.

10

When the centipedes have had their fill and followed my command to leave, I cover Hannibal's body—what's left of it—with rocks. It's the closest thing I can get to a burial.

I wish my father were here. No—he would be disappointed. He didn't kill another human being until the whole world was at war. He would have found another way. Would have controlled the centipedes better. I've only been here for a matter of days. Of course, if my mother were here, she would have done the same thing. She'd pat me on the back and tell me to move forward.

But I can't. Hannibal is dead because of me. He was evil, sure, and he meant to kill me first. But despite serving the Nephilim, he was still a human. He could have been redeemed. Nephilim simply cease to exist when they die, because they don't have souls. But Hannibal had a soul.

So instead, I wish for my brother Samuel. He would simply sit and listen. He would understand. He wouldn't judge me. And he would help me figure out what to do next.

Something I have to figure out on my own.

I take a deep breath and put a hand on Moses for strength. There were three hunters who escaped the centipedes. I'm sure they went back to Freya, to tell her about my powers, and to face whatever punishment Nephilim dole out for failure.

But if they've gone back to Freya, I can track them. And hopefully, they will lead me right to Aquila.

I climb onto Moses's back, and together we swim across the river to pick up their trail.

We travel for a day and a night. I think. It's hard to tell in the underworld, where the sun doesn't rise or set. But since we only stopped once to sleep, I'd say that's about right.

That first night, my dream changes. I'm still in my bed, deep in the castle. But when the silence is disturbed and a creature sneaks in, it's not the Nephilim I've come to expect.

It's Hannibal.

I sit up in bed and stare at him.

"You," he hisses. But his mouth doesn't move. His thick, rough voice is in my head, echoing.

You. You. You.

For the first time ever in this dream, I have the courage to speak. "I am not weak," I whisper.

"You killed me," he says. The words are like black fog in my mind. "You are not your father's daughter. You are one of us."

I wake up with those words echoing in my mind.

One of us.

What does it mean? They roll through my mind, over and over, throughout the day. One of them. One of the hunters. One of the Nephilim servants. The thought makes me sick.

But maybe—maybe it's true. I am not good, like my father. I am not brave, like Aquila. I am cunning, fierce, brutal. And I am a coward, more willing to kill someone than to risk my life to save him.

Moses stops with a jolt. I grip his neck to keep from falling off. "What is it?"

His head is raised, as though testing the air.

I sniff and listen. The scent is suddenly familiar.

I cry out in happiness and surprise. "Zuh!" I clamber off Moses's back and see her emerging from an opening in the tunnel wall. I run to her, forgetting myself until I'm within reach. Then I stop short and look her up and down.

"It is good to see you alive, Norah." She reaches a hand out toward me. She's not much of a hugger, but isn't beyond a pat on the shoulder. Still, Aquila was taken by Loki. A shifter.

"How did you find us?"

"Us?" She frowns.

"Me and Moses. Uh, I mean, the cresty." I gesture behind me, where Moses watches warily. "It's okay, Mose. She's my friend."

But Moses doesn't move any closer. I shrug and turn back to Zuh.

"So how'd you find us?" I look her up and down. "How'd you get better so fast?" I have so many questions, but I slow down to let Zuh respond.

"I tracked you. It wasn't too hard—you left quite a trail." Zuh smooths down her pouf of hair and grins at me again, but the comment stings. "As for the healing, I used Nephilim blood."

"*What?*" My hand lowers toward Smite. "You told us to *never* touch Nephilim blood."

She nods. "And for good reason. Undiluted, in a wound, or your mouth, even your eye, it could send you into a frenzy, or kill you. But thinned in water...it can heal. There was more than enough blood in the jungle, and the rain diluted it enough. It is painful, though. Excruciating. But it works quickly. You can ask your father about it when we get home."

"*He* used Nephilim blood to heal?"

"In the years leading up to the War for Antarktos, most hunters did. It was fairly common back then. Most considered it an honor, to have such raw power in their veins, if only for a short time. I did not enjoy the experience, but I am alive, and here to help."

She reaches out her hand again, and this time I step into it. She puts her arm around me and pats my shoulder.

I step out of the partial embrace, fighting the urge to wrap my arms around her waist. "I need your help."

Zuh frowns. "You still haven't located your sister?"

"I lost the trail a couple of times." I seethe with embarrassment. "And I had some run-ins with hunters. They're tracking me, trying to kill me. They said they served the goddess Freya. Have you heard of her? Do you know where to find her?"

Zuh shakes her head slowly. "No, but I know *who* she is. A bulbous, hideous thing with a hooked beak. She's the Norse goddess of fertility."

Understanding furrows my brow. If she's a goddess of fertility, that means Freya is a breeder—a Nephilim who gives birth to all sorts of monsters to do her bidding. "What does she want with Aquila?"

Zuh squints at me as though sizing me up. "I don't know, but Aquila would make a good bargaining chip when dealing with your father."

My stomach sinks. "You think they want a ransom? What will they ask for?"

Zuh crosses her arms, and her voice drips with anger. "Freedom. Power. They've been hiding in the dark for so long, their power stolen and their pride destroyed. Your father crushed them. They have every reason to be angry with him."

I shudder at her words. "You think...they'd make him give over Antarktos?"

Zuh's countenance turns dark. "Giving up Antarktos would mean giving up his life."

Moses doesn't like Zuh, I can tell. It bugs me. Sure, she's got a harsh edge, and she kind of smells from the journey through the underworld, but she's my friend. She's the one best equipped to help us save Aquila.

I try to remind him of this as I stroke his head, but he doesn't seem to get the message. He keeps watching her with a strange look in his eyes—almost like fear. The muscles in his shoulders haven't relaxed since she got here.

"It's okay, Mose," I whisper again.

Zuh looks up from where she sits cross-legged on the ground, building a fire. "How did you tame the cresty?"

The edge in her voice startles me. It sounds...hungry. Dangerous. Moses's tension must be rubbing off on me, because I avoid the true answer. "I fed him."

Zuh frowns as if she doesn't believe me. "And he didn't eat you along with the meal?"

"I've always told you—creatures like me. I'm nicer than you are, and I don't wear a scary chain around my chest." I smirk at my insult, but Zuh doesn't. I stare at the kusarigama wound around her body and frown. "Where did you find your weapon?"

Zuh looks at me and then down at the chain, confused. "I found it lying in the jungle, discarded in the branches. It's no way to treat a good weapon."

Zuh strikes the flint and steel again. I've never seen it take her this many tries before. She must be really stressed. A shower of sparks lands glittering on top of the heap of dried animal dung. It lights, and the cave seems to stretch awake with flickering reflections and shadows. "Loki was a fool to leave my blades behind."

"Isn't he the Norse trickster god?"

Zuh nods.

"He must be working for Freya, then. That means she has more than just hunters on her side." I stand and pace up and down the tunnel. Moses watches me anxiously. "But if he's a trickster god...maybe he doesn't really have an allegiance to any side? He just likes to make mischief. Create chaos."

Zuh nods again, grinning. "Sounds like Loki."

Maybe there is a way to sway Loki to our side, I wonder. *At least for a short time. Maybe we could even use his help to rescue Aquila.*

After a brief rest, we set out again. Zuh lets me take the lead, watching and no doubt evaluating as I follow the scent, but it's apparent she knows these passages well. I wonder what things she has faced down here and what battles she's had to fight. I've only been down here a few days, and already I've faced more life-threatening situations than any of the past years combined.

"You want to find dinner tonight?" Zuh asks, as she hikes by my side. The tunnel is too small here for us to sit on Moses's back, so he trails behind us, ducking his head.

I place my feet carefully on the rocky slope, trying not to slip. "You know the tunnels better than I do. And you know what's best to eat."

"But you've got the way with animals. Moses is so devoted that he'd probably let you eat him."

I glance at Zuh. From the look on her face, I don't think she's kidding. "Moses is my friend."

Zuh shrugs. "That's a lot of fresh meat."

I frown. "We can find food somewhere else."

Zuh shakes her head. "If you can get a cresty to obey you, perhaps you could find another animal willing to sacrifice itself."

Zuh is right—I *could* get an animal to come to this tunnel right now, if there're any nearby. I think of calling out an animal and killing it, and the image brings me back to the scene by the river: Hannibal, covered in blood, dead on the ground. I shudder.

"I don't like killing."

"We must all kill to survive." Zuh sharpens the blades of her knife against each other, the ringing sound echoing down the tunnel. Moses grumbles.

I didn't have to kill Hannibal, I think. My eyes well up, and I turn away. The voice comes back into my head. *One of us. Weak. One of us.*

Which is it? I want to scream. *I don't want to be either!*

There's a noise up ahead of us in the tunnel. Zuh and I stop short, and Moses does the same with a quick gesture from me. Holding up the crystal, I see something moving. A creature, about two feet long. It has a pointy nose and is covered in patchy gray fur. Its eyes are white, as though it hasn't seen the sun in a long time.

"The animals just come to you, don't they?" Zuh smirks. With a quick whip of her hand, and before I can say no, a chain flies through the air. Its knife tip impales the creature's side, staking it into the ground. The rodent-like animal stills, its limbs flopping.

"Zuh!" I cry.

"You want to eat, don't you?"

A rush of guilt fills me. I summoned that creature just by thinking about it. Accidentally, sure, but it was my fault all the same. His body is limp, blood seeping onto the ground. Like Hannibal looked on the shore. I choke against tears, refusing to let Zuh see. Instead, I let her see me nod. Disgusted as I might be, I *do* need to eat.

"You'll be hungry once you smell this one cooking. You go over there and skin it—I'll stay back here with Moses and build a fire."

I stare at her for a moment, angered that she would ask me to do such a thing when I'm clearly upset about the creature's death. But that's also classic Zuh, forcing us to face our fears and beat discomfort into submission. Still, this hardly seems the time or place for such a harsh lesson. But I agree anyway, wanting to show her my strength, which seems to have faltered since reuniting with her.

I head down the tunnel and set to the miserable task. The creature's skin piles up on the floor around me. He's little, with not a whole lot of meat on his bones. He must be some sort of burrowing creature that lives underground. I feel the urge to name him, but I know if I do, I won't be able to eat him. And like Zuh said...I have to survive.

"Sorry, friend," I whisper. "I'm so sorry."

An animal scream of anger and pain echoes down the tunnel behind me. "Moses!" I shout, leaving the rodent and scrambling up the incline to where I last saw Zuh and Moses. The crystal's light waves against the walls, and that's when the two shadows come into focus: Moses, backing into the tunnel wall, and Zuh with chains outstretched and swinging —aiming for his head.

11

I command Moses to duck his head just in time. Zuh's kusarigama sweeps over him, missing by inches.

"What the *hell* are you doing?" I scream. I picked up the words from some of father's military friends. He wouldn't approve of me saying them, especially not to our revered Zuh, but right now I'm so angry that I don't care. "I told you to leave Moses alone!"

Zuh glances at me. The ferocity in her eyes startles me. She swings the chain again, but Moses can't see it. He's looking at me.

"Duck!" I yell, leaning back as though pulling him.

Moses moves faster than seems possible for a beast his size, and the chain barely scrapes the side of his neck. He roars again and swings back around to Zuh. His mouth opens, teeth pointy and glinting, and he moves to bite her.

"Stop!" I scream. "Both of you!"

Moses stops. His whole body strains with anger, but it is as though an invisible force is holding him back. Zuh lets the chains drop beside her and smiles.

"You *do* control him," she says. "I knew it."

I suddenly realize what this was—a test. How dare she? Moses senses my anger and lurches forward, but I pull him back.

"I knew you couldn't let him hurt me," Zuh says, taunting.

"What were you trying to do?" I growl.

"You were hiding this from me," she says. "You're like your father. Connected to Antarktos." Her voice is full of hatred, and the words *your father* sound like an insult.

I pause. Zuh has never spoken that way about my father before. As much as she sometimes disagrees with him, and especially with my mother, she always reveres him. Yes, it's in her own proud way—the hunter way—but she would never speak of him with hatred.

I stab the air with Smite. "Get away from me!" My body shakes with anger and the exhaustion of holding back Moses. "I don't want to speak to you."

"Still so weak," she says and stalks off down the tunnel.

I hear the sounds of flint and steel. Soon the taunting scent of meat wafts up the tunnel. Still I sit resolute with Moses by my side, stroking him until he calms down.

But on the inside, I'm chaos. Zuh is the one person I can rely on outside of my family. As much as our stubborn personalities cause us to butt heads, she is my supporter. She has always been there for me. And this is a dark side of her I've never seen before. What did I do to bring this out? Did something else happen to her in the caves, or perhaps when Loki attacked her? *The blood,* I think. *She used it to heal, but perhaps it affected her personality, too.*

When I fall asleep, one hand on Smite and one on Moses's side, I find Zuh and Hannibal at the foot of my dream-bed, chanting over and over.

One of us.
One of us.
One of us.

Zuh and I walk in silence for hours. I refuse to let her ride Moses, even when the tunnel is plenty big enough, and when I'm not riding him, I stay by his side. I know she attacked him to test my powers, but she's lost my trust.

The trail continues at a downward incline. We pass through a few clearings, where we find vegetation and animal life, as well as some still pools. These provide the perfect opportunity to rest and refuel. We also wiggle through some tight spaces which Moses only goes through at my urging. I know Zuh is watching, but I ignore her.

She doesn't seem to care. In fact, she seems to be enjoying it. She doesn't offer to help track the hunters' scent, but instead carries herself with an obstinate pride. I quietly rage.

And then the seething turns to worry. What's going to happen if we find the enemy and we aren't on the same side? If the blood she used to heal did affect her, how do I know she won't turn on me or Moses? How are we going to get Aquila out alive when we don't even know what we're facing?

I stop at a fork in the tunnel. There are three offshoots, two stretching downward, with one small crevice in the center leading upward. I search for signs of disturbance, but the trails are equally scattered, and the scent clings to the mouth of all three. It's as though the hunters split up...or distorted their trail on purpose.

"We've lost the trail," I mutter to Zuh without looking at her.

She moves forward, inspecting the tunnels.

She looks overhead, squinting at the entrances, thinking. "I recognize these tunnels. The path most likely to lead to Freya is the middle."

I frown at the small opening, which will certainly be uncomfortable to burrow through. "And why's that?"

"Trust me."

"I don't." I cross my arms and stare her down.

She glares back. "Have you ever heard of Valhalla?"

I shake my head slowly, unwilling to admit she might know more than I do.

"It's Norse legend. The location of the afterlife for deceased warriors. Part of, but separate from, the underworld."

"Like Tartarus?" I ask.

She nods. "Rumor says it's down there somewhere." She motions to the small tunnel. "And no one goes down this tunnel for fear of it."

"Freya is Norse," I say. "She could be hiding there. And if it's like Tartarus, my father wouldn't sense her presence."

"Exactly." Zuh smiles at me, but it's really a mocking grin.

I grunt and push past her, running my hands along the rock. Then I shake my head. "It's too small. How would Nephilim get down here?"

Zuh shrugs. "I'm sure there's another tunnel, but this is the only route I know of."

"Moses can't fit through here. We're not leaving him behind."

"What about Aquila?" Zuh asks. "You wouldn't abandon your sister for...this." She glances at Moses.

"We'll...just go another way."

"You can't rely on the strength of others forever."

I clench Smite so tightly that my fingers feel numb. "The scent leads down all three paths." I march ahead to the left, following the road more traveled.

But Zuh is right.

After several hours of hiking and backtracking, both of the larger tunnels are dead ends and a total waste of time. By the time we get back to the fork, I'm sweaty and more than a little cranky.

"Look where we are," Zuh says.

I ignore the sarcasm and head toward the crevice. "I'll go first, then."

Moses grumbles at me, and I run a hand along the smooth scales of his forehead. "It's alright, Mose. No one's going to hurt you." I glare at Zuh. "I'll make sure of that."

She just stares at me, one eyebrow quirked, waiting for me to move.

I hoist myself up into the tunnel. Loose stone grinds into my kneecaps and palms, but I slide forward slowly. Crawling upward on hands and knees in a tiny tunnel is not an easy feat. Almost right away, the tunnel narrows. I'm going to have to suck my stomach in for this one.

"It's tight," I call. "Are you sure this is safe?"

"Don't let fear stop you," Zuh calls back.

I slide Smite through first. Then I wiggle my arms and head through the opening, but it isn't quite big enough for my shoulders to slide through. The rock tears at my armpit, and I grit my teeth against the pain.

"You through yet?" Zuh's voice is muffled, but I can still make it out.

"Not quite," I grunt. I can't get enough air into my lungs to speak loudly, so I'm pretty sure she didn't hear me.

If I'm having trouble with this tight squeeze, how will Zuh fit? I've heard that some hunters had ribs removed, broken or reshaped so they could fit through tighter squeezes, but Zuh isn't one of them.

I wiggle for a couple minutes, trying to slide through. Finally, I manage to get past my shoulders. My armpit is streaked with blood. But the rest of this should be easy, because my shoulders are the widest part of me. I slip through and collapse into a more open space.

"Zuh?" I call.

It's quiet behind me.

"Zuh, you can come up now."

I peer back through the tunnel. She hasn't even gotten into the crevice yet. If I tilt my head just right, I can see the top of her head, fluffy with dark hair.

"Zuh!" I call louder.

I see a chain flying. And then I hear Moses roar.

"Zuh!" I yell, throwing myself back into the tight rocky opening, trying to grind myself through. But with one arm behind me and one stretching forward, I'm stuck. I wriggle violently, ignoring the pain of skin ripping off my back and arms. "Zuh!" I lift my head and see the knife come down—right into Moses's head. His roar fades, his eyes darken, and he falls. The cavern shakes.

I scream.

12

Zuh's face appears at the end of the tunnel. She's leering at me, and her eyes are filled with more venom than I've ever seen. This isn't the Zuh I know.

She's been corrupted, I think, *by the blood.*

She killed Moses.

I lose control. I scream and spit and wave my arms, trying to hit or hurt or scratch her with my nails. Smite is stuck behind me in the passageway, and my only weapons are my hands. But she's too far away. So I throw my body forward with as much force as I can. The rock pulls against my shoulder before letting me free, and I hear a clunking sound as the bone dislocates.

I scream as it wrests free, and I lurch at Zuh, falling out of the tunnel and knocking us both to the ground. I flail on top of her, punching her face, clawing at her eyes. With a free arm, she swings a chain around me and uses it to roll me underneath her. Her eyes gleam with evil, corrupted intent, but her hair is still black. Not even a streak of red. She holds her knife over my face. We're both breathing heavily now. I have no weapon and my shoulder pulses with pain. Out of the corner of my eye, I see Moses's limp body. Furious, burning tears rise to my eyes.

"I thought you were my friend," I hiss.

Zuh laughs. "You thought wrong." She lowers the knife to my throat. "They were right. You *are* weak."

Nausea swims up my throat, and I fight back the sudden urge to vomit. "Who was right?"

"Your sister. Your mother. Your father."

The words are like daggers in my gut, twisting, cutting me open.

"You're lying." I don't believe what I'm saying, and we can both hear it.

"You're a coward," she spits.

"Better a coward than a traitor."

A slow grin spreads over Zuh's face. "To each his own."

"What are you going to do to me?" I stare up at her, fighting the urge to look away, to run from the fear of death. "Why?"

"If it were up to me, I'd kill you," she says, pushing the blade into my skin. "And I'd enjoy it."

Kill me? Zuh? Red hair or not, she *has* been corrupted by the Nephilim blood, reverting back to her old ways before my father set her free.

"Who's it up to, then?" I will not look away. I will not back down. I will not show my fear. But my heart is in my throat, pounding, spilling blood down the small slice in my neck.

"Weak *and* stupid," she says, and she follows up the two verbal punches with a third. "I serve Freya."

The word is spoken with reverence, and my blood turns cold.

"You've been working with her this whole time?"

"A little hair dye and an occasional smile at the right time goes a long way," Zuh says.

"That's why you were gone for so long? After the battle for Antarktos?" I pause, as I realize something I had never considered before. "You weren't *hunting* Nephilim, you were helping them *escape*."

A smirk. "Freya wants you alive. You're connected to the continent. You have abilities that she thinks will be...useful. We thought Aquila would be the best for the job. No surprise. Your sister is daring and brave, unlike you. But she hasn't shown any supernatural connection to Antarktos. Not like your father. Not like you." She pulls the knife back from my neck a little, and I gulp in air.

"So whichever one of you proves best, we'll keep. The other...well, I'm sure we'll find some use for you." Zuh grins and stands, jerking me by my dislocated arm. I yelp in pain. "Get up!"

I stand, shaking, blood dripping onto the floor around me.

"Back into the tunnel," she says. "Try anything and I'll yank your other arm out of its socket."

I think of Smite sitting inside the tunnel waiting for me.

"Your hammer is mine now," she says.

"Smite." I glare at her. "Its name is Smite."

"Start moving." She shoves me forward, and I stumble, body screaming. Before I hoist myself up into the crevice again, I look back for one final glimpse of Moses. Blood drips down the center of his pulverized forehead, but his face is calm, as if sleeping. I have the urge to run back, to cry over him, to stroke his wounded forehead and bandage him up. To apologize for not keeping him safe like I promised. But it won't do any good.

Zuh shoves me again.

I turn away and pull myself into the tunnel.

The passage is narrow and difficult to squeeze through. Crystals line the walls and pull at my raw skin. But I do not cry or complain. Zuh is always right behind me, prodding me forward, and I'm determined not to show weakness. Because I am *not* weak.

I will not be.

I will be my father's daughter.

Thoughts of him keep me going. He was only a little older than me when he was captured by hunters and forced to do unimaginable things. He was broken by them, and had his sense of self stripped away. At least I still have that. I can still think for myself. I haven't had my memories torn from me, haven't lost all the things that make me Norah Vincent, daughter of Solomon, King of Antarktos.

A memory plays in my head, the same one I'm forced to revisit every night in my dreams, and I feel the familiar fear rising up. I wouldn't mind having that memory taken from me. The fear is what makes me weak. The fear has changed the brave, fierce, relentless Norah into the girl I am now. The girl who weeps at death, who flees from danger, who prefers to pretend the underworld doesn't exist.

Yet here I am. Hundreds of feet underground, fighting and facing death even though I don't want to, even though I'm afraid. My skin is stained with blood and my eyes sting with the urge to close, to sleep. But I am still moving–moving closer to my sister and my fate, whatever it may be.

I am Norah Vincent, and I will not let the Nephilim take that away from me.

The tunnel widens, and for the first time in a while, I am able to stand. My legs are shaky, and I put one arm against the wall to hold me up.

Zuh follows and stretches her legs. Smite is wound tightly in her chains against her chest. She smirks at me.

"Looking a little tired there."

I force myself to stand up straighter and drop my arms to my side. "I'm fine."

"Stubborn as usual. Refusing to admit your own weakness."

I look away from her and up at the tunnel walls, trying to act as if I don't care.

Something flies across the tunnel and hits me in the stomach. I grunt and step back as Smite falls to the floor in front of me. I stare in disbelief and look up at Zuh.

"Pick it up."

I crouch slowly and wrap my hands around the handle.

"Now's your chance. Fight me. Give it all you've got."

Something's wrong with this situation—I can see it in her eyes. She knows something I don't. She's not afraid. She's grinning, waiting for me to strike.

So I do.

I step closer and take a swing at her side. The chain whips around and catches my arm, twisting my aim. I stagger to the side, holding onto Smite for dear life.

She doesn't hesitate. She whips the chain again and knocks me off my feet.

I lay on the floor, sweating, breathing heavily. Fresh blood pours from reopened wounds. As I stand, a wave of dizziness crashes over me.

"You look weak." Zuh leers at me, eyes bright with pleasure in my pain.

I lurch forward, hammer sagging, and she pushes me away with a hand. My skin burns with shame and fever. There is no way I can win this, and she knows it. I close my eyes and take a deep breath.

"If you wanted to kill me, you would have done it by now," I say.

"Oh, but you miss the point, little one. I just want you to see how weak you really are." She stands in front of me, arms outstretched. "You couldn't kill me even if you wanted to. Even if I put a knife into your hand." As she says this, she unwraps a chain and hands me the end with the curved blade attached. "Go ahead."

I look at the knife in my shaking palm, and I look up into her eyes. They are the deep brown eyes I am so familiar with, but they are filled with malice. She hates me from her core. I can see that now. She hates my family. She hates the freedom of Antarktos. And she will not stop until she brings me to my knees.

To give up now would mean weakness. She wants me to use her own knife against her, but she thinks I am too weak. Too kind, too innocent, too afraid to kill.

What she doesn't know is that I have already killed.

I wrap my fingers around the knife. They aren't shaking anymore.

And then I stab the knife into her chest.

13

Blood oozes out from around the wound. My eyes widen in shock, not because I've stabbed my old friend and protector in the chest, but because her blood is purple. I release the blade and pull my hand back.

Zuh takes hold of the knife sticking out of her chest. She draws it out, slowly, letting out a moan of pleasure. Then she beams at me, delight and power filling her eyes. The purple blood trickles down, and the wound grows larger, expanding. She feeds off the pain like it's energy.

Next she laughs and rolls her shoulders, which seem to be growing larger. The skin stretches open around the wound, large chunks flopping to the ground. Red scales glisten beneath the surface, as Zuh's body molts away. It's like she's growing from the inside, expanding to twice her size, shedding her human skin and revealing scales the color of raw flesh underneath. Skin and broken chains lie in a heap on the ground.

The last remains of Zuh slough away, leaving a ten-foot-tall monster with red scales, glowing yellow eyes and horns.

While the sight of this thing fills me with revulsion, I am also relieved. This isn't Zuh. Never was Zuh.

"Loki."

The monster bows his head.

"What have you done with Zuh?" I yell.

"Tasted her blood," the shifter says. "So sweet. Taken from the full sack of an insect. Then I left her for dead in the forest. I assumed you would die, too, without her protection."

"*You* took my sister." I shake Smite at him, as if it will do any good.

"Freya needed her. But you, my dear, might be an even better fit for the task at hand."

"And what is that?"

Loki looks me up and down. "Eh, I still think Princess Aquila is the better choice."

"For *what?*"

Loki sighs. "Don't you know by now what we Nephilim want, what we have been planning since before you were born?"

The look on my face clearly says I do not.

He shakes his head in disappointment, and then he grins. "The assassination of your father."

I can barely stand by the time we reach the gates of Valhalla. When Loki told me his plan, I lost control, lashing out, kicking and screaming. After a thorough beating, he wrapped Zuh's chain around me, keeping me from fighting anymore. He laughed in my face. I spat on him. He then knocked me unconscious and carried me for who knows how long. When I woke, I considered calling more centipedes to my aid, but I don't want to be responsible for any more deaths.

So I walk.

The chains are heavy, and my skin is more bruises and blood streaks than anything else. My muscles shake, but I keep my chin high and my back straight. I am Norah Vincent, daughter of Antarktos. I will never be Loki's conquest. I will not show weakness. I keep telling myself those things, over and over, as he marches me toward the gates.

The huge, arched doors are constructed from stone slabs run through with veins of gold. They're built in the wall of a vaulted cavern. Strange creatures prowl before the gate. They have wings like an eagle's, and hooked talons that click on the rocky floor with each step. But their heads and front legs are those of wolves and their bodies are covered in thick red fur. Their eyes are beady and pale. They snarl as they see us approaching, revealing sharp, yellowed teeth.

"What are they?" I whisper.

"The guardians of Valhalla." At Loki's booming voice, the creatures bow their heads and skitter backward.

They recognize him. They obey him. I feel sick to my stomach.

Loki shoves me forward, and I trip, hitting the ground face-first, unable to stretch out my hands and stop myself.

As the throng of wolf-eagles—*weagles*, I decide to dub them—bark at us, I roll over on my back and stare up at Loki. "You're a Nephilim. Why do you serve Freya? Aren't you equals?"

Loki sneers. "I *serve* no one but myself. The army needed a figurehead." He looks away from me and starts to rant. "Freya was once a laughingstock. The Nephilim warriors adored her, but I don't see why..."

I start edging away, scooting on my butt. I know I can't make it far, especially with the chains weighing me down. The weagles glare at me, but I don't want to face whatever's behind those gates.

"She hates me," Loki says. "I told her she was a flirtatious whore after she slept with every warrior available. Breeders don't even need to copulate. She's just..." His shoulders shake. "Ugh."

My own eyebrows go up in shock, and I fight the urge to laugh, as Loki continues with his story.

"Even my twin had his way with her." A snicker. "Of course, he's dead now. Thanks to your father. Not that I mind."

I'm still smiling. The idea of humor is out-of-place in such a desperate situation, but I'm beyond exhausted, and I'm seeing a whole new side of my captor. This whole thing seems ridiculous—running around underground, eating cream-cheesy centipedes, befriending dinosaurs, killing someone I thought was my ally and finding out she was actually a *he*—an evil trickster Nephilim? I shake against the laughter, and the chains jingle.

Loki whips around, and I see the anger in his eyes as he discovers I've been edging away. "Get back here, you little—"

I fumble to my feet, turn, and run.

"Get her!"

I hear the sound of clicking talons on the ground, and then wings. The weagles are after me. Just the thought of that name—*weagles*—almost makes me start laughing again. But no, I have to focus, I have to run. I can't let him take me...

An image pops into my head. Me, a knife in my hand, stabbing it into a person's chest. Stabbing my father.

One of us.

Suddenly I'm gasping for air, sweating, all laughter gone from my face. This is what I will be forced to do if I'm taken by the Nephilim. If they break me. This is what I will become. An assassin responsible for my father's death. And if I don't help Aquila...that's what she'll become, too.

Talons dig into my swollen, bloody shoulders, and I cry out. The weagle flings me to the ground. The pack swarms around me, growling, yellow teeth looking huge and bright against their dark blood-red fur.

I hold my hands open, even though they're chained by my sides. "Don't eat me, please don't eat me," I beg.

The growling subsides. The lead weagle, the one who caught me, cocks his head. I feel a surge of relief. Even these strange creatures obey me. *They must be Antarktican*, I decide, though who knows how they got roped into being the guardians of Valhalla.

I lay my head back on the ground, breathing heavily, ribs straining against the chain. Fresh pain pours through my body, as I lie on the cold, hard floor. I can hear Loki's footsteps stop beside me, but I make no effort to move. *I could kill him,* I think. With a pack of weagles following my commands, I could have him torn to pieces. I could escape. And I nearly make the request. But then my thoughts turn to Aquila, trapped behind those doors, and I know what I have to do.

He reaches down and grabs my dislocated shoulder, jerking me up to my feet. I cry out in pain.

"Only the weak run," he hisses.

I square my one good shoulder and glare at him through the sweat stinging in my eyes. "I'm not running. Not anymore."

14

The weagles open the gates for us.

As I turn to face whatever lies ahead, I have to blink against the light. It's brighter than any of the crystal-lit caverns to which my eyes have become adjusted. But when the pain of light subsides, I see Valhalla. It's...a banquet hall, lit by low-hanging chandeliers. The longest table I've ever seen in my life stretches down the center of the room, laden with heaps of food and steaming meat. After so many days underground, the scent is incredible. My stomach practically screams at me to dive in. But what I see seated around the table holds me back.

Hunters. At least a hundred of them, all with thinning red hair and lined faces. All corrupt. All old. And all glaring at me.

My stomach sinks. These must be Hannibal's friends.

"Looks like the little lassie is getting what she deserves," one spits at me. He eyes me up and down, taking in all my bruises and blood streaks.

A kick to the back from Loki sends me to my knees. My dark blonde hair falls in front of my face, but I feel the pink flame rising in my cheeks. To them, I have been subdued. I look weak. I'm humiliated, but I clench my jaw in determination and force myself to stay down. I have to bide my time. I have to do whatever it takes to save Aquila.

A loud chirping noise echoes through the cavern. All heads turn toward the sound. I look up and see what my hunger-driven eyes didn't notice the first time.

Sitting at the far end of the table, I see...a blob. A fifteen-foot-tall heap of skin and fat, collapsing in on itself like a melting pile of whipped cream. And at its apex, it has a face—what looks like it might be a woman's face, but with a beak instead of a mouth, and feathers sticking out of the top of her head. Its beady black eyes glare down at us, the double—make that triple—chin vibrating as it chirps. Small nubs wriggle at its sides. *Hands,* I realize. The thing's arms have been enveloped by its girth. This creature is by far the most disgusting thing I have seen in the underworld, and it's not hard to identify.

A breeder.

Freya.

When she finishes, another voice takes over. But I can't hear it with my ears. It's inside my mind.

I see you have returned, Loki, and with the girl.

Panic squeezes my chest as though the chains are trying to strangle me. I know that voice. I hear it every night. But this time, it's real.

Shaking beyond control, I look around the room, searching for the voice's source. There, standing at the fat bird-woman's seated feet, I find him. A Nephilim called a gatherer. The monster whose luminous, penetrating black eyes I have seen over and over, tearing through my mind. His egg-shaped head is too big for his thin insect-like body. He should be comical, but all I can see are his eyes. Looking into me. Looking deep inside my mind. And I am terrified.

My fingers reach for Smite, but the weapon still dangles from Loki's chest. In my mind, I'm a little girl again, without weapons and sitting in her bed, helpless, staring at the creature whose voice echoed and melded with her own. *You are weak. I have seen your mind…*

"I have obeyed your orders, Freya, but on one condition." Loki's voice resounds in the hall, and I frown.

Freya gives a few clipped, angry chirps.

The voice pushes into my mind again. *And what is that?*

I breathe again, as I understand. The gatherer is translating for Freya. And the voice isn't just coming into *my* mind—Loki can hear it, too. Probably everyone in this hall can, judging by the attentive looks on their faces.

"I want to bring her to meet her sister. Give them a little...reunion." Loki smiles as though being generous, but I know that smile. It's one of evil intent. His eyes glimmer with the same malice I saw in the fake-Zuh's eyes. I wonder how I fell for his disguise for so long, how I didn't know she wasn't my Zuh. *I'm so sorry, Zuh.*

Freya pauses, then chirps again. The mind-voice sends her message. *Fine. Try not to let the older one harm her sister too severely. I want both of them intact.*

Loki jerks me to my feet with the end of the chain. "Come."

I stumble, legs shaking. Actually, my whole body is shaking. My mind feels like a hand has groped through it, broken down its defenses and sifted through my insides. It hurts, and not just physically. If the creature has paid any attention, he knows my fear. He recognizes me. He has the power to bring me to my knees—to find and expose the weakness inside me.

I'm quivering so much that I can barely walk. I move only because Loki is shoving me along.

I have to block the gatherer out, I realize. I have to block them all out. Shut down my mind, shut down my defenses, act like I am confident and strong. I pull my shaking shoulders back and hold my head high, staring straight ahead of me as I walk around the table, behind the row of hunters. I feel their glares. And then they start mocking me.

"Three cheers for the Princess!"

"So small."

"But she'll look delicious with red hair."

You are weak, the memory of the voice echoes.

I am not weak!

The voice forces its way into my mind again, cutting through my defenses with all the pain and power of a bullet. *I know your weakness. You will not last long here. Breaking you will be a simple thing.*

Panic sets in again. It's his voice. Real, this time, filled with spite.

I turn and look, to see him staring at me, empty eyes threatening to suck me in.

No one else is looking. No one else can hear it. Just me.

He found me.

He knows my weakness.

He knows I'm afraid.

Loki opens a door in the side of the hall and pushes me down a set of dark, narrow, stone stairs. Unable to catch myself with my arms chained to my sides, I tumble down. It's so dark that I can only tell which way is up by the parts of my body not hitting the floor. Every bruise reawakens and screams with pain. I cry out, and Loki laughs.

"You're not going to feel any better when I'm done with you," he says.

Splayed on the rocky steps, covered in the scent of blood, all I want to do is curl into a tiny ball and hide. To pretend I'm not really here. To shut out the pain. To not face Loki and whatever evil thing he has planned. Maybe if I close my eyes tightly enough, I can pretend I'm back home, in the gardens, sunlight on my face...

A sharp kick to my side jolts me out of the vision. I scramble to my feet and continue down the stairs, out of the reach of Loki's feet.

At the bottom, a locked door awaits. The keys hang on a hook outside the door. I frown, then realize it's a prison cell. Is this where they're keeping Aquila?

The gatherer's warning, on behalf of Freya, slips into my mind. *Try not to let the older one harm her sister too severely.*

Did they break her? It's hard to imagine, but many of the strongest people I know—my parents, Zuh, Aunt Em— were once broken. *Would she attack me? Kill me?*

Loki unwraps the chain from around me, and I shake one sore, beaten arm, trying to restore blood flow. I'm afraid to move the dislocated arm, so I just massage it gingerly.

"You're going to need this," Loki says, throwing Smite at me. I catch it this time. An overwhelming sense of relief fills me as I hold its handle, my only real piece of self-defense. Then comes fear as I realize: Loki wouldn't give me my weapon unless I really did need it. Unless something bad was about to happen. I clutch the weapon tighter.

Loki takes the keys and unlocks the door, ushering me through, ahead of him. It may be the first gentlemanly thing he's done on this whole trip. The room is cool and dark, and I think I hear the sound of breathing.

My eyes haven't even adjusted to the dark before I feel a solid blow to my ribcage.

"Oomph!" The air bursts out of my lungs, and I stumble backward. With my good arm, I swing Smite out in front of me blindly, hoping to hold off my attacker until my eyes adjust.

I hear Loki chuckling.

I squint, and something comes into focus. Someone small. Someone with light eyes and...red hair.

No...

Oh, no...

"Hello, sister."

15

"Aquila!" I nearly sob in relief. My sister is alive, but is she still my sister? Her hair is blood red. The hair of a broken girl, remade as a corrupted hunter, like those in the great hall above. I decide that knowing is worth risking injury. Dropping Smite, I take a step toward her, arms outstretched. But she steps back.

"Aquila," I say, voice trembling. "You are not one of them."

"I am no longer called Aquila," my sister says. Her offensive poise is familiar, but her face is harsher than I've ever seen. The excited, inviting look I am so used to seeing in her eyes is gone. "I am Aimee, servant of Freya, Goddess of the new Nephilim."

The use of Aimee's name—Aquila's middle name—in service to the Nephilim enrages me. Aimee, wife of Merrill Clark and mother of Mirabelle Whitney, single-handedly saved our father from serving the Nephilim, freed him from his corruption and prevented Nephil from possessing his body. In the world of Antarktos, her name carries the same weight as George Washington once did in the United States. She is a hero, and like a grandmother to us.

Aquila's muscles are more rugged than they used to be, more visible against her thin arms—perhaps because she's stronger or perhaps because they haven't fed her enough. Her skin is streaked with blood and grime. She moves toward me with more precision and focus than I've seen before. I scuttle backward and hit the wall behind me. The fear returns, as I realize she's right. She's *not* Aquila. She's someone else.

My dislocated arm hanging by my side, I pick up Smite and hold the weapon in front of me. At least I still have my right arm. For the first time in a while, I find myself praying. *Please, please don't make me hurt my sister.*

A blade flicks out of Aquila's hand, glimmering between us. Strike. The tip is two inches from my face when she whips it to the side, gesturing me away from the wall. I move slowly, gripping Smite with all my strength.

"Fight me, Princess," she spits. "Let me show you what Nephilim hunters are made of."

I force myself to breathe. Focus. I just have to keep her from hurting me, and try not to hurt her.

She jabs forward, and I deflect the blade with the head of my hammer, spinning it away from me. She lunges again, and I parry. She twists, spins, brings the blade down against my cheek and leaves a shallow slice. I inhale as I feel the sting across my skin, the warmth dripping down my face.

She cut me.

She made me bleed.

She swings again, but this time I duck. As the movement carries her away from me, I slam Smite down on her foot.

It makes a horrible cracking noise, and I hear her pained croak.

I think I just broke all the bones in my sister's foot.

The sound of it replays in my head, and I nearly vomit with disgust over what I've done.

Aquila doesn't leave me time to linger on it, though. She swings again, downward, and I fling myself to the side. The whooshing blade narrowly misses my head, but manages to slice off a few inches of my hair. The blonde strands fall limp to the floor, another thing severed between us.

I scuttle backward along the floor, trying to regain my feet, but she keeps swinging at my legs, and I have to keep pulling back.

"Aquila!" I shout in frustration.

"That's not my name!" she shrieks, and with that she bends down and grabs my leather shirt. She picks me up and presses me to the wall with one hand, the other holding Strike to my throat. She stares into my eyes for a long moment. Blue eyes into brown. Sister into sister. In that fleeting instant, I wonder if she sees herself in me. If she sees the person she was.

"Hesitation is your weakness," she hisses, her voice so low I can barely hear it. *What?* What is Aquila—Aimee—saying?

Then she shoves me against the wall again, draws Strike back, and aims the tip at my heart.

Without thinking, I swing Smite up and knock the sword out of her hand. I use the momentum to swing back around and release the hammer, throwing its head into her gut.

She gags and falls back, sliding across the floor toward Loki's feet.

I snatch Strike off the ground and stand above her, pointing her own sword at her throat.

Then I look up at Loki, defiance and anger in my eyes.

But he's smiling.

"I can see you two have some things to work out," he says. "And as much as I would like to watch the anguish of this confrontation coming to a close, Freya wants me to keep you both alive."

He walks over and pulls me off of Aquila. Aquila, glaring, stands up and dusts herself off.

"You've just made yourself an enemy," Loki says, chuckling.

"She's not my enemy. She's my sister."

"Not anymore." Loki pries Strike out of my hands and tosses it at Aquila's feet. "You humiliate a hunter...you make an enemy for life."

I'm left in a cold, dark cell, much like Aquila's. Loki told me to save up my strength for what is ahead. What that is exactly, I don't know. All I know is that I'm in pain everywhere. My skin stings every time a new bruise touches the floor. My head aches from exhaustion, from the intruding voice and from one too many blows. My dislocated shoulder. My aching feet. My muscles hurt from walking, and my stomach hurts from hunger. I can't help but think of the banquet above, the hunters sitting around enjoying their bounty. They have food. Chairs. Light. Warmth. Things I would give anything for right now.

Well, not anything. I think of Aquila. It's worse than I thought—the Nephilim *have* broken her. I touch the scab on my face, the dried blood crusting my pale skin. Compared to all of my other wounds, this one hurts the least—but it sparks pain inside me that I don't want to face.

My sister, my biggest defender, the strongest, bravest, most valiant person I know: she did this to me. She fought me. Hurt me. Made me bleed.

I wince and close my eyes. How am I ever going to stand up to the Nephilim if my sister couldn't?

I fumble in my pouch for my sketchpad and charcoal. It's all Loki hasn't taken from me. I twist the charcoal in my fingers, watching the stains it leaves behind. Black. With just one touch, my hand is unrecognizable.

What did they do to her? What did they do to change Aquila into Aimee, to destroy the sister I know and love?

And what did they do to me, that I was willing to break my own sister's foot? How long will it be before *my* hair turns red?

I flip the sketchbook open, and I stare at the blank white page. In my head, I see those empty, dark eyes staring back at me. And I know what to draw with the charcoal and the black stains on my hands.

I draw until I fall asleep, the gatherer's eyes gazing at me from the page, reflecting the darkness of my own soul.

A hunter wakes me up with a blade pressed against my throat.

"Good morning," he says, voice rough and breath hot on my face.

He's going to kill me. He's going to avenge Hannibal's death, right here in this cold, dark cell.

"What do you want?" I whisper, holding very still, so the blade doesn't slip and open up my throat.

"I *want* to kill you," he says.

I was right. I run my hands along the ground, looking for any sort of weapon. All I find is a stick of charcoal.

"But Freya wants you alive. For now." He pulls the blade back. "Get up."

He shoves me, and I stand, following him out of the cell, up the stairs and back into the central hall of Valhalla.

But the scene in front of me is entirely different from yesterday's. The table has been pushed to the side of the room, clearing a wide central space up and down the hall. A ring of hunters lines the walls, hooting and yelling at something in the middle. The hunter who woke me grabs me and pulls me through the wall of people.

In the center of the ring, hunters are fighting. Some are facing off in pairs, while some are clumps of hunters whaling on each other like a gang fight. Every time someone gets a good hit, hunters around the room whoop and holler.

Over all of this, Freya presides, sitting in her lumpy, stately fashion at the end of the hall. Though it's hard to tell exactly through the layers of fat distorting her features, she looks...pleased.

A hunter falls to the ground screaming, his arm landing beside him, dismembered. This gets a terrifying cheer from the crowd. I feel sick to my stomach.

Freya chirps, and the gatherer's voice follows: *Halt*.

It takes a minute or two for the voices to quiet down and the punches to stop being thrown. Many of the hunters look angry at this interruption.

We have a new participant here today.

Eyes search around the room and land on me, standing uncomfortably on the inside edge of the circle, the hunter gripping my arm. A holler starts up again, some words I don't understand, but it sounds like they're booing me.

Loki, bring her weapon.

Loki, who's standing next to Freya, nods and takes Smite from his belt, handing it to the gatherer.

The gatherer nods to Loki and scuttles down into the ring of hunters, who part to let him through.

I freeze as I watch him coming closer and closer, his eyes dark, sucking me in, just like the eyes I drew before I fell asleep. When he is right in front of me, he stops, his spindly front legs balancing Smite atop them with what looks like impossible strength.

He looks into my eyes, and the thought that comes next is for me and me alone.

You and I both know you cannot win this.

He holds Smite out to me, offered like a gift. But I know it is more like the knife prepared for a sacrifice—this hall is the altar, and I am the slain.

I take Smite in shaking hands and stare the gatherer down.

My name is Soren, he tells me. *You can stop referring to me as 'the gatherer'.*

How did he—? My heart is racing. He knows what I'm thinking. He knows how much I fear him.

Soren turns and crawls back to his place beside Freya.

Release the warrior, Soren orders.

Warrior? But—my father destroyed all the warriors. There shouldn't be any left. My heart races as Loki walks to a giant door at the side of the hall and enters. The hall is dead silent, and I hear the jangling of keys. He's letting something out.

The crowd hears it, too, and they shout in excitement. The hunters in the center of the ring draw back to the outskirts, leaving me alone and feeling very small in the open space. My palms are almost too sweaty to hold on to Smite, so I wipe them on my shirt one at a time.

Then a massive creature in a loincloth stumbles out of the open door. It's twenty-five feet tall, with gangly limbs and a drooping belly. It looks like a man, but huge, ugly and disproportionate. Tufts of red hair pock its body. Its eyes are blank, as though in a stupor, and its jaw hangs open. Its footsteps shake the hall as it moves, limbs swaying, dumb eyes searching. This isn't a warrior. This is a slow-witted monster.

"Where?" it mutters, the word slurred. "Where izz see? Where izz food?"

Loki points at me. "There."

The shouting grows louder. The beast swings his head, and his eyes fix on me. "See...small," he says, frowning in disappointment.

Taking deep breaths, I try to harness my panic. I will not be food today. Aquila needs me. Yes, this monster is huge—but he's also stupid. If I can't out-fight him, I can at least out-smart him.

Then the voice butts in. *Fight her,* Soren says. *She is your food.*

Hunters around the room pick up the chant. "Fight! Fight! Fight!"

I lift my hammer and hold it steady in front of me. I can do this, I tell myself. I can do this.

No, you can't.

I whip around to see who else heard, but only Soren's eyes are on me. Everyone else is yelling at the monster, spurring him on.

I can.

You are weak, Soren says. *You are weak against the darkness inside of you. You think you can hold it back, but you can't. It terrifies you. So you run away. But you cannot run away from it forever. It will always come back to haunt you.* He pushes farther into my mind, and I can feel him turning over memories, looking at my nightmares, staring down at Hannibal's bloodied corpse. *Just like I come back to haunt you every night. Just like whenever you think you are happy, whenever you think you are free, you will see Hannibal's face in front of you and know that you can never be happy. You can never be free.*

I stumble backward. The monster is moving toward me, one heavy step at a time. I'm still holding Smite, but it feels incredibly heavy. My arms shake.

You are weak because you refuse to grasp your true strength. You ignore the darkness and so lose your greatest asset. Deep down, you are more ruthless than any of us, but you run from it.

I want to run now. But the monster's eyes are fastened on me, and the ring of hunters feels as though it's closing in. There's no way out.

I know you remember me, Soren continues. *I know you think about me every day. You know why I came that night, don't you?*

I frown and sweat breaks out on my forehead.

I don't know.

Suddenly the answer's absence paralyzes me. I have never stopped to ask *why* Soren came for me. Why my mind was the one that he chose to uproot and torture.

You want to know why? The cold voice slithers in my mind, taunting me. *Freya sent me. She wanted to know which daughter would make the best killer. I took one look at you and knew you didn't have it in you. You are not a fighter. You are a coward. Afraid, even of your own potential. You will always be running. Running from the darkness, running from your fear.*

I've edged backward so far that I've almost reached the end of the hall. I stop, with nowhere left to go, a hundred hunters who want me dead surrounding every possible escape route, pushing me forward, rough fingers against my back.

Freya thinks we can break you. Soren smiles. *But I think you will simply turn into a sniveling mess.*

The giant monster swings a meaty hand down at me. I block it with Smite, swinging out with my one good arm, but the blow is feeble. The hammer is nearly yanked from my fingers. The Nephilim wrings his hand, as though it stung but didn't do much further damage. Trying to go on the offensive, I use the move that worked in my last fight: aiming for the foot. But my hammer doesn't even make contact before I'm scooped up and dangled fifteen feet in the air.

The Nephilim grunts, looking down at me in his hand. His eyes are as big as my head. "I am warrior. You are puny girl." His thumb presses painfully into my middle.

I flail against his grip, slamming my hammer down again and again, making glancing contact with his fingers and his wrist. But he just squeezes me tighter.

I take the deepest breath I can, my ribs aching against the restraint of his hand. Then I tense, and with all my might, I throw Smite at his stomach.

The blow hits hard and accurate. The monster staggers backward, dropping me from my fifteen-foot-height. I brace myself and collide with the floor on my hands and knees. All the weight goes on my good arm, and the wrist snaps and screams with pain. I stand and grit my teeth, resisting the urge to cry out. Now both of my arms are incapacitated. A kind of strange numbness fills me as the joint swells.

The monster regains his balance and focuses on me again. His dull eyes are angry now. He roars and takes a step toward me, but I dodge him, running in a zig-zag and retrieving Smite from the floor. My wrist screams as I flex my fingers around the handle, but I ignore the pain. My wrist might be broken, but my arm and fingers still work. Then I dart between his legs. He turns around to find me behind him. Then he roars again, frustrated.

I wind up Smite for another throw. Then I hear the voice.

Your hair is turning red.

Smite falls from my hand as I fumble through my hair, more afraid of corruption than I am of death. "Where? Where?" I pull the closest strands in front of my face. Still blonde. I shake my hair over my eyes, trying to see if the hair in back has turned red.

And then, when I can't see, a hand grips me. Tighter this time. I scream as a rib pops.

"Stupid girl," the Nephilim grunts.

I shake my hair out of my face and turn, searching for Soren in the audience. He lied. I should have known, but I let my fear guide me. I let *Soren* guide me. I kick with everything I have, weaponless and defenseless.

The Nephilim squeezes harder. My insides feel as if they are about to burst. Everything in my middle is turning into a fiery red mass. Without consciously choosing to, I scream louder than I ever have in my life. The sound is inhuman.

The voice is what saves me.

Stop.

The monster stops, his hand relaxing slightly. My scream subsides and fades into weeping.

Bring her to me. Your master Freya needs her alive.

I feel every lumbering step the monster takes, ripping through my body. I hear myself sobbing as the monster places me on the ground in front of Soren.

Take this weak one to her cell.

It's the last thing I hear before human arms scoop me up, and I black out.

16

I'm running. Everything around me is dark, and I can't see where I'm going. But I know what I'm running away from. The voice. It's echoing around me as though we're in a huge cavern. I'm in the underworld. The air is clammy and cold. My body pulses with pain. Each heavy breath I take cuts at my throat and pushes against a stabbing pain in my side. But I keep running. The voice gets closer and closer.

You are a coward.

My chest heaves, but I'm not getting enough oxygen. Panic starts to spiral through my brain, and I feel dizzy, disoriented.

You are not a fighter. You are a coward. Coward. The words repeat, over and over, louder and louder.

I can't fight back. I know somewhere in my gut that what he is saying is true. I *am* a coward. My feet tell me this as I run, tapping out the drumbeat of my fears. *I am. I am. I am.*

You will always be running, the voice says.

I see a light in the distance and I move toward it. My eyes might be playing tricks on me, but I don't care. Maybe if I reach the light, I can escape the darkness that surrounds me.

The light grows, and as I reach it, the scene changes. I'm in a dimly lit room—a room I recognize. The bed in the center is my own. But for once, I'm not the one in it. I see Soren at the foot of the bed, and I see a lump under the covers. Someone is in my bed.

Soren isn't looking at me—he's looking at the lump. This gives me the courage to move closer. I stand at the edge of the bed and pull back the covers. What I see makes me too terrified to scream.

A limp body lies in my bed, face mangled, red hair soaked in a puddle of blood. His blue eyes are open and empty. Dead.

I stagger back a few steps, hands over my mouth. "Hannibal," I whisper.

This is the darkness inside of you.

I turn to Soren, whose enormous black eyes are fixated on me now.

Stop running and give in. Give in to the darkness, Norah.

The eyes get bigger and bigger, and as I open my mouth to scream, the darkness swallows me.

I open my eyes, panting and struggling for air. Every breath makes my ribs spasm in pain. I look around me, frantic. But I'm not in the vast darkness or my old bedroom. As my eyes focus through the dim light of the underworld, I see where I am. I'm in my cell.

Alone.

Smite leans against a wall, close, but still out of reach.

I breathe a heavy sigh of relief and force my muscles to relax. And as my breathing quiets, I hear something I didn't notice at first. A scraping sound. Coming from the door.

Panic grips me again, and I try to push myself up. But my right wrist collapses under my weight. Pain radiates from the spot and fills my whole body. It takes everything I have not to cry out.

I remember all that happened before I passed out. The fight with the monster. Getting brutally beaten. My wrist is broken, and judging by the pain in my chest, at least one rib is, too. And I haven't forgotten the ache of my dislocated arm.

I lay back against the cold floor and try to keep my breathing quiet. At this point, it's all I can do. I can't get up. I can't fight. So I resign myself to the reality of the situation: a hunter is probably outside that door, ready to break in and kill me for what I did to Hannibal. And I will have to let him.

Deep down, I know it's what I deserve.

Something clicks in the door, and it is heaved open, the stone grating against the floor. I hold my breath and close my eyes for a brief moment. Then I turn my head to face my death straight on.

I see the glint of a sword, and then a spiral of light as it coils in on itself. There's only one sword I know that can do that.

Aquila limps into the room.

Fear courses through me. Last time I saw my sister, she wanted to kill me. I open my mouth to speak, but in a rush, Aquila is by my side. She clamps a hand over my mouth and holds a finger to her lips.

"Shh."

Her head is up, cocked toward the door, listening. I listen, too. Nothing. She looks down at me and meets my eyes.

The hatred I saw in them last time is gone. The playfulness I once knew is gone, too, but what I see now, I recognize. It's the look of my older sister watching out for me, asking me to trust her.

I give a small nod, and Aquila nods back. Then she stands and moves back toward the door, pushing it shut.

"We still need to stay quiet." She kneels beside me and starts pulling supplies out of a bag by her waist. "I figured you'd need some medical attention, so I found what I could. There's not much here. Fortunately for us, the hunters store centipede guts in jars." She holds up a sealed canister and wrinkles her nose. "You look worse than I thought."

"How did you..." I trail off, staring at her. I must be imagining this. Aquila was Aimee. Aquila was evil.

She sets the jar on the ground and holds up Strike. "Picked the lock with this. The Neph aren't very smart. They put a lock on your door and leave you with a weapon." She shakes her head. "They need to raise their standards for testing who is broken, and who isn't."

"They didn't? Break you?" I hear the doubt in my voice, and Aquila hears it, too. She stills.

"Almost. But not quite. I don't think it works as well when you know what they're doing. And I'm sorry about that fight. I didn't want to hurt you, but I had to keep up the ruse."

"You really did a good job acting, then." I speak slowly as I think of the malice in her eyes, the sister I hardly recognized. "And I'm sorry for breaking your foot."

Aquila winces, but then nods. "It helped Loki believe what he was seeing."

As I stare up at my sister, a thought occurs to me— a question I'm frightened to ask. But I have to know. "Your hair?"

Aquila reaches up to touch the red strands. "It's blood. Mine. I cut my hand and ran it through my hair as a disguise. See—you can feel it. It's dried."

I touch her hair and find that it is, in fact, crusty with blood. "That must have been hard to do."

"Only because I have to keep on doing it. Blood turns brown after a while." Then she shrugs. "But you've suffered through worse, it seems. What happened? Where are you hurt?"

I tell her about the fight with the monster and name my injuries. I tell her about my journey through the underground—avoiding the story of Hannibal's death—and I tell her about Loki being disguised as Zuh. She nods as though she already knew all about that. As she listens, she takes charge of the situation, splinting my wrist, rubbing centipede ooze into any open abrasions, and assessing my dislocated shoulder. She definitely paid more attention in Zuh's lessons than I did, because she seems confident as she tends to my wounds.

"I'm going to have to put it back in place," she says, standing above me and reaching down for my hand. I notice she keeps her weight off of her broken foot—the foot I broke. I swallow back the guilt.

"It's going to hurt, but it will be worse if I don't."

I nod and close my eyes tight. "Do it."

I feel her hands around my arm, and then a wave of pain as she pulls my shoulder with a quick burst of force. The bone slides up and into the socket. I cry out, and we both freeze. Listening. But no one responds to the cry.

"They probably expect you to be in a lot of pain right now," Aquila whispers.

"They'd be right," I say through gritted teeth. The pain is blinding for five solid seconds, and then, it fades to a dull ache. I move my arm, happy to see it is once again fully functional.

Aquila bends over my arm, prodding it gently. "I think it's all set."

I nod, unable to form a thankful response.

"You said the monster squeezed you, right? You might have internal bleeding." She pulls my shirt up from my stomach and sucks air in through her teeth.

"What? What is it?" I struggle upright, using my now mobile left arm.

She points at my stomach. Beneath the skin, a red and purple bruise swells, bigger than both of my fists put together.

"Is that internal bleeding?" I ask.

"I think so." Aquila looks more worried than I've ever seen. She's usually confident, and her worry scares me.

"Oh, Quil..."

"It's okay. You're going to be okay," she says. "You just need to rest and not move much. I'm going to watch out for you. Okay?"

"But the Nephilim..."

"Need you to heal." She reaches for the jar of centipede flesh. "Eat some of this. It will help."

I swallow a few bites, fighting intense nausea. My mind plays out all the ways I could die. Skewered by a hunter's sword. Crushed by a monster's fist. Starved and bleeding to death in this cell.

"How do you know I'm going to be okay?" I ask.

She looks at me, pursing her lips. "I'm not sure if this will make you feel better or worse..."

"What is it? Tell me."

"Do you know where we are?"

I frown. "Valhalla."

"Yeah. And Valhalla isn't exactly *in* Antarktos."

"Like Tartarus," I say, remembering a similar conversation with phony-Zuh.

She nods. "It's underneath Antarktos, sure. But it's another realm. It's like...a supernatural place. You remember the Norse mythology, right? They believed that Valhalla was the afterlife. That it was the place great warriors went when they died, carried here by Valkyries."

My eyes widen. "Are *we* dead?"

Aquila shakes her head. "No, no. It's not like that. The hunters here are basically retired. They got too old to carry out normal hunter duties, and the Nephilim honored them by bringing them here. Not that they have selfless motives—they kept these hunters for backup, in case of war."

"But you just said they're old. Won't the hunters die soon?"

Aquila shakes her head, slower this time. "No one dies in Valhalla."

"How is that possible?"

Aquila shrugs. "It's another realm, like I said. It's not the afterlife—it's an eternal place, outside of time, I guess. Except, unlike Tartarus, the Nephilim like it here."

"So...we can't kill the hunters here."

"Or the Nephilim."

I sink my head back onto the stone. Not only are we trapped here—we're trapped here forever. We won't die. And neither will our captors.

"You know what they want to do with us, right?" I ask in a hoarse voice.

Aquila nods. "Father."

That one word sums up everything we have to lose. Everything Antarktos has to lose.

"We have to escape."

Aquila snaps Strike open. "Already have a plan."

17

"Tell me about Freya," I say.

We're hunched in one of the tunnels outside of our cells, which will bring us on a roundabout route to the storage room. I've got Smite, clutched in my left hand, the arm still sore, but feeling strong once more. Aquila needs to return the medical supplies—including the now half-empty jar of centipede goop—to their proper places, and we have to put the plan in motion there.

"She's very fat," Aquila whispers.

"I knew that."

"Right. But it gets better. She's so fat that she can't move."

My jaw drops. "Are you serious? How does she eat?"

Aquila makes a face. "She sends out a pheromone that attracts centipedes. They crawl up her, and she swallows them whole."

I shudder. "If she can't move, what good is she?"

"She's a breeder, and a breeder's main job is just that: giving birth to feeders. New Neph. There's nothing she does that isn't gross."

"Were you in a feeder pit?" My whisper sounds both disgusted and horrified. Feeder pits are where the Nephilim break hunters. A breeder situated high above the pit gives birth to feeders—dumb, hairy baby monsters with sharp teeth—and the person in the pit has to kill and eat them to survive, before they themselves are killed and eaten. Over and over, until something cracks. Usually a skull, or a soul.

"I was in a pit...but not a feeder pit. Freya's not birthing feeders. She's birthing these strange monsters. They're bigger than feeders—anywhere from five feet to fifteen feet tall. They grow, too, if they're allowed to live." Her voice darkens.

"What do they look like?"

"Men. Men with monkey arms and huge stomachs. Nephilim-red hair. I call them baboons—it makes them mad."

"That's what tried to kill me," I say. "That's what the Nephilim made me fight."

Aquila nods. "Testing your strength. I wonder why they didn't just put you in a feeder pit. But I've never seen one as tall as the one you described. It must have been birthed long before I got here."

"Why is she birthing them? Why'd she let the baboon I fought grow so big?"

"Weapons, maybe. They're stupid, but they're big. I think..." I can see Aquila's frown even in the dark tunnel. "I think they're building an army, hoping that with Father gone, they'll be able to take over."

"We won't let that happen."

Aquila shakes her head. "No, we won't."

We continue down the tunnel, cautious, keeping an eye out for any Nephilim or hunters wandering around. But it seems they are all in the great hall, as expected. Aquila says they're on a schedule. They start off the day eating and drinking and laughing around the table together. Then someone gets drunk and says something bad about someone else. Before long, the table is shoved aside and a huge fight breaks out. After one side of the debate has been squelched, the hunters realize they're hungry and they pull out the table again, where food has miraculously reappeared. The hunters with wounds nurse them, humiliated, and the winning hunters gloat. Eventually they are so full and drunk that they fall asleep, and when they wake up, the cycle starts again.

Apparently Aquila figured this out by listening to the waves of shouting and laughter coming from above her pit, and she was able to put it all together when the Nephilim thought she was broken and brought her out into the great hall. The hunters had cheered when Soren announced her as 'the hunter who will assassinate Solomon, traitor and mass murderer of the Nephilim!' It was then that Aquila had realized their plan—and then that the defeated hunters rushed in, telling of the attacking centipedes, Hannibal's death and their failure to kill me. This news had given Freya pause. The returning hunters were banned from Valhalla for their cowardice in fleeing from a little girl, and Loki was sent after me. Meanwhile, Aquila continued her plan: to act like a broken hunter and wait for me to come, so we could escape together.

It's incredible to me how well she has been biding her time, how carefully she tricked the Nephilim. And now we're nearing the first step of her plan. With Aquila beside me, I don't feel so afraid.

"I'm going to go in first," she whispers. I nod and wait as she pushes the storage room door open just a crack. No light or sound comes from inside. We enter quietly and shine a crystal around. Shelves surround us, and a table sits in the middle of the room. Empty platters and pitchers sit on the table. Aquila returns the jar and the supplies to their respective places. In case something goes wrong, we don't want Aquila to be found out. If they knew she wasn't broken, things would be much worse.

"Let's find the strongest alcohol in here." Aquila starts opening and sniffing bottles.

I frown. "How do we know the drink will get to them?"

She stays focused on her task. "Somebody's got to bring the food and drink out there. They come in and out of here all the time—look, you can see the worn path on the floor."

I look down, and she's right. The stone has been smoothed away where many feet have moved over it. It seems like a flimsy plan to me, but what else do we have? Two wounded girls can't take on a hundred hunters.

"So we just fill the pitchers with half regular wine, and half something...much stronger. We just want to make sure they're out cold when we make a run for it." She holds up a canister, sniffs it and takes a swig. "This should work."

"Aquila!" I chastise. "Father doesn't like for us to drink."

She squints at me. "Father probably doesn't like for us to get kidnapped either."

I frown at her.

"Anyway, it'll give me a little extra oomph for this job, and make me forget the pain in my foot. You want some?"

"No, thanks."

We pour the drink into the empty pitchers and mix it with wine, so it looks about the right color. We're setting the canister back on the shelf when something bumps outside the door. Both of us freeze. Aquila sets the canister down quietly and waves for me to hide between the shelves. I jump into the hiding spot before I realize there's nowhere for Aquila to hide. She stands her ground, Strike outstretched, as the door heaves open.

A gatherer takes one step inside and freezes. At first I think it's Soren, but then I realize this creature carries himself differently. His head is hung low, as though he's a slave, and his legs are even more spindly than Soren's. His eyes bulge out of his gaunt head.

And then he sees Aquila. Something flashes in his eyes, and his mind-voice calls out: *Intruder—*

He's cut off by Aquila's sword, slashing through both of his eyes.

He writhes in pain, but he doesn't make a sound. There's no scream of pain searing through our minds, no call for help to his fellow gatherers. He's upset—but pain doesn't make Nephilim upset. Pain gives them pleasure. This gatherer is distraught, and it's not because of the pain. It's as though, by damaging his eyes, Aquila has taken his voice.

Aquila turns to me. "The others will be coming soon. We've got to run."

I nod and jump out of my hiding place, following my sister to the door. She stops before we exit and turns to the gatherer again. His eyes are mending themselves, as Nephilim wounds do. So Aquila slashes them again and bends over his wounded form.

"Tell the others that the daughters of Solomon, the rightful King of Antarktos, will bring judgment on all their kind."

Then she chops off both of his spindly front legs, and his body collapses to the floor, wriggling helplessly.

She coils Strike and pushes me through the doorway, limping behind me.

I hear feet behind us. It's a clicking sound, like a huge insect is tapping against the floor, racing toward us. I turn and see at least ten gatherers scurrying down the hall. Excluding their alien eyes, they really do look like insects. I freeze, my heart in my throat.

Aquila grabs my arm and pulls me, leading me down the hall away from them. We're fast, but the gatherers are faster.

We're not going to outrun them.

I can't get enough breath in my lungs to tell Aquila, or even shout for her to stop. But I don't have to. The gatherers do it for me.

The mental attack comes hard, like a cold tidal wave slapping my body and carrying me off my feet. By the terrified look on her face, I can tell Aquila feels it, too.

It's not words or sly deception like Soren uses. It's pure despair groping through our minds, settling over everything. My memories and thoughts are churned through, without any clear purpose except to exhaust and confuse me.

The despair is enough to stop us in our tracks. I don't realize I'm standing still until I look down at my feet. Unmoving. Surrendered.

The gatherers surround us. I notice halfheartedly that Smite is lying by my feet, but I make no effort to pick it up. I blink and Hannibal's face appears, glowing, behind my eyelids. Shame settles on my shoulders like a heavy blanket. I turn to look at Aquila, and it feels like I'm moving through a fog, like my head is a heavy metal weight sitting on my shoulders.

What I see reflected in her face is different from what I'm feeling. I see anger there. And hatred—the hatred I saw in her eyes when she fought me. But this time, it's different. Her blue eyes are big against her abnormally pale face—big and crazed.

She unsnaps Strike from the palm of her hand and spins in a half-circle, red hair flashing, and she fells five gatherers by chopping their legs in one swoop.

The weight of the despair settled over me releases just a little. In the moment of clarity, I pick up Smite, using my splinted wrist to support its weight, and I slam the nearest gatherer over the head. He collapses and struggles to regain his feet. Again, the mental hold over me weakens.

Go for the eyes, I think. I see the gatherer's eyes widen as he reads my mind, just before I hit them with all my might. He crawls backward, helpless, waiting for his crushed eyes to heal.

I take out a second and a third gatherer before I turn to see what Aquila has done. Before me lies a ring of blinded, dissected gatherers. Spindly legs coated in purple blood spatter the ground, amputated from their owners. Already

I see new flesh growing from the wounds. A puddle of purple blood oozes out toward my sister's feet.

"Aquila, look out for the blood!"

She turns to me, panting, chest heaving, eyes wild. Her face looks like it has been spattered with tiny new freckles. I squint and realize they're purple.

The blood is on her face.

"Oh, God," I breathe.

And then Aquila pushes Strike up against my throat.

18

"Quil," I breathe, not daring to move.

She pushes in closer, eyes narrowed. I catch my breath as Strike's blade digs into my skin. How many times have I had a knife up against my throat in the last few days? I try not to count.

"Aquila," I say again. "What are you doing?" My voice quivers. Is she pretending? The gatherers can already tell she isn't broken. She wouldn't have cut them down if she was. But now...there's Nephilim blood on her face. Nephilim blood that has the power to kill a person.

"Power," she says, looking beyond me. "I feel...alive."

"That's adrenaline," I say. Zuh—or rather Loki disguised as Zuh—had said that undiluted Nephilim blood, if in a small enough dose, would not kill you, but would give you a rush of adrenaline. A sense of power beyond its ability to heal. It's like it speeds up all the body's systems, including the recovery system, and it increases emotions. Like anger.

She focuses on me again, blade held rigid.

I shut my mouth and close my eyes. She couldn't kill me even if she wanted to. Not here, not in Valhalla. Right?

A clicking noise echoes down the hall. My eyes snap open. Aquila turns to look, distracted, and I whip my arm up and knock Strike out of her hands. It clatters to the ground between us. We both dive to the ground, but I get there first. I turn the sword back on my own sister, holding it level with her chest. She stares at me, eyes wide, angry.

Good job. The mocking words echo in our minds. Both of us turn our heads to look at the source, but I know who it is before I see him.

Soren. He's found us.

You've turned on each other. Congratulations.

"No!" I yell. "It's the blood. It will wear off."

Soren shakes his head. If I knew how to read emotions on an alien-like face, I'd say he's grinning. Laughing at us.

We've broken her, he says. *She's no longer your sister.*

"No," I say, but less emphatically this time. "She's faking. She's not broken. You *never* broke her."

A repulsive grating sound, a laugh I think, fills my mind. It feels like it's shredding my insides. I shudder.

All it took was a little violence to push her over the edge.

I look around the hallway. Limbs and purple blood litter the floor. The injured gatherers are starting to stand on newly grown legs, their mostly-healed eyes shining with wrath. I feel their angry buzzing enter my mind. My head aches, and I begin to feel dizzy.

Quiet, Soren orders. The noise diminishes.

"No," I whisper.

Look at her hair.

I look at my sister. She's angry, I can see that, but something is holding her back. It must be Soren. Her red hair frames her face, flyaways sticking out in all directions. I reach out to touch a strand. The crusted blood flakes away in my hand, but the strand is still red. Soren is right.

I stifle a sob.

The gatherer voices swell again.

Bring them to Freya!

They must pay!

They ought to be cast out and killed—

Silence! Soren orders again. *Freya doesn't need to know.*

A wave of confused words that I can't decipher fills my mind.

The next wave of words from Soren is painful. *I am in charge! Anyone who disagrees can leave Valhalla to wander until they die.*

The gatherers quiet.

Now take them to the pit.

Spindly arms take Smite and Strike before I can react. Then a gatherer has grabbed me and lifted me. Next to me, Aquila struggles in the same predicament. Corrupted maybe, but still looking for a fight. I'm dragged through the hall and into a narrow, dark tunnel. The ground sways below me, and I feel the rising urge to puke.

The pit.

The feeder pit. The pit where baboons are born, where hunters are broken, where we will become our father's assassins. Where Aquila will have no one to stop her from hurting me.

We stop at the edge of a black hole in the earth.

Throw them in, Soren commands. *They won't die.*

And then I'm hurtling through darkness. My chest is tight. I can't breathe. Everything slows down, and I wonder if this is what dying feels like.

Then I hit the ground. Pain bursts through my whole body. Stars dance in my vision and blood rushes to my head. For a moment I think I'm going to pass out, but I don't. I wish I would. The silence would be merciful. Death, painless.

Above us, the voice echoes, distant and yet clawing directly into my mind. *No food will be coming.*

The clicking of gatherer feet resounds in the air and then dies away.

Aquila stands beside me and shrieks. It surprises me. The pain made me forget she was here, too.

The noise is animal. Her whole body is shaking, as she cries to the sky, waiting for an answer that won't come. Through the dim fog of consciousness, I wonder if she is having some sort of horrible reaction or withdrawal from the Nephilim blood, now that its strengthening effects have worn off.

That probably means she isn't very safe to be around. I move my arm around on the ground, looking for Smite. I breathe a sigh of relief when my hand collides with the familiar handle. They left us with our weapons.

Then I realize that may not be such a good thing. They're leaving us like gladiators to fight in the pit... Only, no matter how badly we wound each other, we will not die.

I stand on shaky legs. As Aquila realizes my presence and turns to me, I hit her over the head with Smite. One blow drops her to the floor, eyes closed, out cold.

I collapse to the ground beside her. With arms shaking from pain, I pull her head into my lap. And as I run my hands through her red hair, picking out the blood and tangles, I let tears slip down my dirty face.

There are bones in this cave.

And worse than just bones—there are faces. I think they're baboon faces, because they look just like the creature I fought—only younger. I wish I could say there were bodies to go with the faces, but there are only bits of flesh and inedible body parts left, clinging to the bones and the floor. It looks like Aquila tore through these corpses when she was trapped in the pit. I grimace at the remains and keep my distance.

It smells like death in here, death and rotting things. I try not to think too much about what exactly is rotting, but I'm reminded of it every time I breathe in through my nose.

And then there's Aquila, slumped on the floor like one of the dead. I did that. *Me.* I knocked my sister out cold. It was for my own protection, sure, but what kind of sister does that make me? What kind of *person*?

I shake my head and begin to worry. Aquila said that the Nephilim had brought her out of the pit. She hadn't clawed her way out like Dad did so many years ago. In which case...there might be no way out, other than help from above. And I don't think Soren's coming back any time soon. He's probably testing us, pitting us against each other, seeing who comes out on top. Seeing who will be the chosen one to kill my father.

I investigate further. The walls are slick and studded with crystals. But what Aquila told me was true: the cycles of laughter and hollering from the hall above vibrate the pit walls and will prevent us from climbing very high before falling back down.

I'm armed with both weapons now—Smite and Strike. I'd be putting my own safety in jeopardy if I leave her sword at her side.

But what am I supposed to do? Battle my own sister? Keep knocking her out until I find a way out? Make sure she's too wounded to fight?

I wince at the thought. Soren is right: my darkness is deep, deeper even than Aquila's.

Yeah, but she's the one who's gone crazy. Not me, I think—and then I feel guilty for thinking it.

"Oh, Quil," I sigh. "I could really use some help right about now."

And then a wild realization comes into my mind. I could call for help. If there are any animals nearby...

I close my eyes and picture the weagles outside the gate. I don't know if they can hear me from this realm, but maybe. I have to hope. With as much will as I can muster, I call the weagles to come in, to enter Valhalla and come down to the pit.

I watch the darkness above me, waiting, hoping. An eternity passes. Maybe the weagles couldn't get past the hunters—although they're probably drunk and out cold by now. Maybe...

After ten minutes, my head hangs low. Despite recovering my sister, I am still alone, and without hope of rescue.

And then I hear the flap of wings.

A weagle swoops down into the pit. It's a dark shape against the dimly lit walls. The wolf-eagle creature settles to the ground before me, talons clicking. Its eyes are frightening and the crusty blood around its mouth speaks of a recent, gory meal.

"Hello," I say. The weagle is bigger than I remembered, and it feels especially big in the closeness of this pit. His head comes up to my shoulders.

The weagle folds his wings against his sides and lies down at my feet, head bowed, deferring to me.

"Stand up," I say. I hold out my open right hand, splint still hugging my wrist tightly. "We can be friends."

The weagle stands and nudges my hand, then licks my leg. It tickles, and I laugh. The sound is strange in this desolate place. It echoes against the walls, like it's mocking me.

"I need your help," I say to the weagle, petting his head. His wolf eyes beam up at me, and he pants happily. "I've got to get out of this pit."

The weagle whines and looks over at Aquila's prone figure. Guilt surges through me. I hadn't even thought about what to do with her. I know I should bring her, but... Visions of her with a sword at my throat make me hesitate.

"I don't think we should bring her," I say, resting a placating hand on the weagle's head. And as I look over at my sister, she stirs.

"Uh-oh," I whisper. The weagle tenses.

Aquila makes a noise and moves as though to sit up. I grab the weagle and pull myself onto its back. It raises its wings, preparing to fly away. *Wait,* I command. The creature pauses. We both watch the girl in front of us as she sits up and rubs her head, then fumbles around her, looking for her weapon, trying to figure out where she is. Then she sees us.

Her mouth curls into a snarl. "You!" she shouts.

I grip the weagle's neck tighter, but I don't give him the order to move. Not yet.

She stands and whips her head around, looking for a weapon, but finding none. "You took Strike!"

She takes a step forward, and I lean back. The weagle shifts underneath me, wings stretching out once more.

Her eyes widen as she realizes what's happening. "You have to take me with you!" she cries.

"You're not yourself, Aquila," I say. "I have to protect you. You tried to kill me."

That's when she spots Strike at my side. I see her processing her options—try to jump us, attack me, take my place on the weagle and leave me here. I won't let that happen. I can't. Fear overcomes me and I push the weagle forward, up into the air. The weagle soars, circling above my sister.

Aquila screams. "You can't leave me here! I am a hunter, servant of the Nephilim! I will not rot in this pit, traitor!"

I know she's not in her right state of mind, but the words sting. I *am* a traitor. My sister has been broken, her personality and her memories and her very self stolen from her, and I am leaving her behind.

But there is one thing I *can* do. I take Strike off my hip, coil it shut, and throw it down to the ground. It clangs against the rocks, and Aquila leaps for it. I push the weagle higher before she can find a way to attack. As he soars up and out of the cave, I look down at her. My sister, alone, screaming with rage.

And then we're flying through the tunnel, back the way we came, searching the bowels of Valhalla for a hiding place.

19

The small cave we find smells musty and uninhabited, so I don't think anyone's been in here for a while. We took as many turns away from the central hall of Valhalla as we could, and we ended up here. I don't even know if we're *in* Valhalla anymore, but I'm guessing that the only way in and out is through the gate. Who knows how big this supernatural realm is. If it really is supernatural, like Aquila says, I'm guessing it doesn't have to physically fit in Antarktos. That gate might literally be the portal to another world. I don't really understand how these things work, but I have long believed in powers unseen and greater than myself. So I don't give the mechanics much thought.

I don't think we could fly out of the gate without all the hunters, Freya, and worst of all, Soren, noticing. So we're stuck in Valhalla, at least until we come up with a plan. And by we, I mean I. My weagle friend won't do much of the planning. I have named him Fenris, in part to honor his Norse lineage, but also because Fenris Wolf was foretold to be the slayer of Odin, and the harbinger of Ragnarok, a time of great destruction that would bring about the end of the Norse gods' rule. Right now, a little bit of Ragnarok would do us good. He's basically a big puppy around me—though judging by his teeth and talons, he could tear a man apart with a quick bite and a shake.

I dismount and pull a crystal out of my pouch. The rock walls here are smooth and mostly bare of crystals, so the light is much needed. I sit on the ground and sigh, head in my hands. Pain that I'd managed to forget floods through my body. My broken wrist aches from the strain of fighting in a splint. My ribs hurt, reminding me that at least one of them is probably broken from the baboon's crushing grip. And although the bruise has faded, my stomach still hurts from whatever damage took place inside there and caused the internal bleeding. At least the centipede flesh I consumed seems to have helped.

Fenris nudges my shoulder.

"I failed," I whisper to the empty cave around me.

Fenris doesn't know what the words mean. He nestles beside me. I let him because I want the warmth, but deep down I know I don't deserve it.

I did fail. I came here to rescue Aquila. Instead, I made things worse. Before I got here, she wasn't broken. She had a plan. She was still in her right mind.

Now I've lost her to the Nephilim. And I left her. I *left* her. How could I be such a coward as to run from my sister when she needed me most?

Tears run down my face. I sniff and wipe them away, smearing grime all over my cheeks, but they just keep coming. I was supposed to be brave and strong. I was once, before Soren got into my mind. Before he destroyed me from the inside out. Before he opened my eyes to my own darkness.

Fenris's presence beside me reminds me of Moses. Remembering him makes me cry harder. Moses died for me. Because of me. Because I couldn't see that his killer was Loki disguised in Zuh's body.

A deep despair settles over me. It feels like the gatherers are overwhelming me again—but this time, I know the voices beating me down are my own.

I've lost Zuh and Moses and Aquila. I'm on my own. And I am not strong enough to face the Nephilim, even with Fenris's help. I'd just get him killed, too. Which means Aquila will become an assassin. My father will die.

Antarktos and the world will fall into the hands of the Nephilim.

Because of me.

I curl up on the ground, head resting on Fenris's side, and cry until I fall asleep.

I'm in my room again.

I know as soon as the dream begins that it's not the same as the others. That the whole night, the one I've fought so hard to forget, is going to come back. And I am powerless to stop it.

I am eleven years old again, and I'm opening my eyes, drowsy, confused. Pain prods through my mind like a finger and then intensifies, stabbing deeper. I put a hand to my head. Am I having a migraine? I squint into the darkness and see a shape. Moving. I freeze, heart pounding out of control. Someone—or something—is in my room.

I want to move, to reach for the hammer at my bedside table, but I can't. I can't get up the courage to move. If I move, it will see me. If I move...

A memory is pushed to the forefront of my mind with shocking suddenness. Me at age five, playing with Aquila, crying when she hit me too hard and me running to Mom for help. Mom frowning at me and telling me, *Stop crying, you're not a baby anymore.* The images are in full color—my mother's wrinkled forehead and disapproving eyes, my sister with her hands on her hips and her indignant voice. *She's so weak.* The sting on my cheek where I was slapped, the red mark I later saw in the mirror that made me cry again.

I didn't even know I remembered that.

I blink into the darkness. The shape is coming into focus. The first things I see are two enormous black eyes that absorb light. The sight makes me catch my breath. I must be imagining this. I must be...

But no. The eyes are set on an egg-shaped head, which sits on a spindly body, a cloak wrapped around its shoulders.

You are afraid.

The words enter my mind without permission. It isn't my voice. Isn't my thought. And it makes my head hurt.

I'm not afraid, I tell myself. *Everything's fine. I'm just imagining things.*

The goosebumps on those skinny little arms say otherwise, the voice replies.

I look down at my arms. They *are* skinny. And they are covered with goosebumps.

My breath lodges deep in my chest. Stuck.

You remember, don't you? All the times your sister made you cry? All the times you quit instead of fighting? You fearful child. You are not a hunter.

"Who's there?" I whisper.

An image comes into my mind. I am somehow outside my body, but I can see myself, and I feel everything. The knife in my chest. The warm blood oozing down my front, staining my hands. The cry stuck in my throat. The copper scent heavy in the air, the scent of the dying. I am dying.

I am dying.

You think you are a hunter, but you are not. If you try to be, this is how you will die, the voice says.

I'm in my body now, my hands on my bleeding chest, my eyes cast down to the wound. And then I look up. Standing in front of me is my sister, eyes fierce, smirking. And I know who put the knife in my chest.

So weak. Her voice echoes in my mind.

I start to cry. In the image, and in real life, my body shakes. The air hurts coming out of my lungs, like I am being choked, like the tears are choking me.

Do you know who I am? The grating voice pushes into my mind again, and the pain makes me want to cry out. I try to fight against the thoughts. This is all in my head. I'm imagining it. It's just dark, and I'm afraid. I'm overthinking. I need to stop thinking and go back to sleep...

I am your enemy. I am the most powerful force on the planet. Your family will pay for what they have done.

No, I think, head pounding. *Go away.*

And you, the voice continues, *you will always be running from me. From my kind. No matter what you do, you cannot escape. You are no hunter. You cannot stand and fight. You are weak. I have seen your mind. You are not what they think you are. You are powerless. Afraid.*

I can fight, I think to myself. *I can fight!*

Then why aren't you picking up your hammer?

The question bounces around the room and fills my mind like a frog's inflating vocal sac. It hurts. I want to scream, to move, to pick up my hammer, but I can't. I'm too afraid.

When I finally lift my eyes, the creature is gone.

That's where the memory ends. That's where the horrible night ended. But it never really ended.

I stir in my sleep, anguished. The despair is smothering me, and I feel like I can't breathe.

It was real. I've tried to doubt it, to write it off as a nightmare. I told only my brother, and he didn't know what to make of it, either. But now I know: it was Soren. Whether or not he was actually in my room is debatable, but him being in my head seems much worse.

Something moves beside me. The dream has not yet ended.

I freeze. This is not a familiar part of the dream. Has the gatherer closed in on me at last? Will it kill me? *Oh God, please let it be quick.*

A hunter must face death with bravery. Reminding myself of this, I draw on every ounce of willpower I have, and I turn to face what is beside me.

I find myself looking into a weagle's eyes.

Fenris is nestled beside me, looking up at me, waiting for instruction with complete trust in his face. He is not afraid. Soren is not attacking him. His faith in my abilities is naïve, but welcome.

His trust gives me courage. I realize that, for the first time in these dreams, I am warm. Fenris's body warmth, pressed up against my side, keeps me warm even in this chilly darkness. And my other side is warm, too.

I turn and see Moses sitting next to me, glaring out at the darkness. It crosses my mind that a cresty's weight would probably break my bed in real life. I almost laugh. The warmth I feel on the outside moves inside, grows and fills me with strength.

The despair lifts, and I know what to do.

I stand and face the dark room. And then I lift my hands, calling Moses and Fenris to stand beside me. Then, together, we step forward.

Before I reach whatever lays in wait in the darkness, before I can hunt Soren down, my hands hit something cold and hard.

The dream dissolves around me, and I blink as I wake to reality.

I'm standing, my hands pressed up against the cave wall. I must have sleepwalked. I can't remember ever sleepwalking before. I turn my head and see Fenris watching me, still curled up on the ground where we slept.

"I just had the weirdest dream," I whisper. "Sorry to wake you." My voice echoes against the walls.

Fenris lowers his head back to his paws, watching me with less concern now.

I turn back to the cave wall, staring at my hands. I can barely make them out in the darkness. The hair stands up on my arms as I think about the nightmare, the rush of strength I gained from Moses and Fenris, and this strange awakening. The cave wall is smooth against my palms. I run my hands down the wall to bring them back to my sides, but I stop when I notice something strange. The wall is smooth—but pocked with lines. Even lines. Unlike the jagged edges of natural stone. Like—engravings?

I hurry back to Fenris and find the crystal lying on the ground. He raises his head again, concerned.

"I think I found something," I whisper, excitement in my voice. He gets to his feet and follows me back over to the wall.

I hold the crystal up, and the light exposes the etching. I was right. Something was engraved here. And that something looks a lot like...animals.

It's hard to identify specific animals, because the engravings are somewhat crude, but I see creatures that are flying and creatures with four legs. I see small creatures and big creatures—mice and birds, lions and giraffes. Elephants. Flamingos. I see what looks like a dinosaur by its long tail and neck. I press my hand up against the dinosaur, missing Moses.

The drawing extends further than the light of the crystal, so I walk along the wall, hypnotized, shining the crystal in all corners. It seems that the animals are gathered in a large circle, all facing the center. They are all looking in one direction, looking at a woman. She stands in the center, arms outstretched, a solemn look on her face.

Is she controlling them?

A shiver runs down my back.

I move further into the cave. Another picture begins. In this engraving, the woman rides on a dinosaur's back.

More animals trail behind her, as if they are following her. This time, the animals are lined up in pairs, an army coming two-by-two. The woman faces forward as if she is moving toward...something. What is it? I hurry along the wall and stop short at a huge image.

It's a boat. A boat with a massive door built into the side, a door that has opened forward and lays on the ground like a ramp. At the foot of the ramp stands a man with a beard. He's looking at the woman, too, waiting for her and the herd of animals to come.

The crystal quivers in my grip. I recognize this image. It's one of the stories my father used to read to me. *Two by two they came into the boat, representing every living thing that breathes...*

In the next image, the woman has dismounted. Her arms are outstretched, and beneath her, animals charge. But they aren't charging at her. They're charging at giant men, who I recognize as Nephilim warriors. The warriors' weapons are drawn, some slicing animals in half, others aimed and ready to strike. Other Nephilim creatures remain in ranks behind the warriors, including the gatherers.

I suddenly know what it would feel like to be the woman in front of the boat. The gatherers pushing into her mind. Telling her she wasn't strong enough to fight.

But her arms are outstretched anyway. And under her command, the animals battle.

Above them, storm clouds are etched into the rock. And a few raindrops are falling, never to land, forever held in that stone sky.

The story continues in the next carving—the most gruesome of them all. Water is rising under the boat. The door is shutting as the last few animals crawl inside. On the top deck, the woman stands, looking out over the ruins as she calls her animals home. The man with the beard stands beside her.

Below them, Nephilim struggle in the water. Some have sunk below the waves, eyes closed, accompanied by slain animals. Others are frozen in the image with their arms flailing, their mouths open for air.

The image extends deeper. Beneath the water, a line is drawn, representing the ground. A series of tunnels spiral underground. Crawling through the tunnels are the surviving Nephilim, seated around a great hall.

I feel sick. Here is where the Nephilim escaped—where they survived. Here is where they've been hiding for centuries: the underworld.

I think this must be the end of the story, but it isn't. One last picture is engraved on the wall. It must have been a different artist, I think, because the lines are different. The story isn't the same. And yet the woman is featured in it.

It's the great hall of Valhalla. I can see that from the massive table surrounded by hunters. There are warriors eating with them, too, so this engraving must have been here for a long time—long before my father exterminated the Nephilim warriors. Freya and Soren aren't anywhere to be seen.

In the forefront of the picture, the woman stands facing a warrior brought to its knees.

And her hand grips a sword stabbed deep into his forehead, penetrating through his skull.

I put a hand over my mouth.

The warrior's eyes are closed. A fatal blow.

But...how? In Valhalla, where no one dies?

When I can pull my eyes away from the woman and the warrior, I search the picture for clues. But all I see is an inscription at the bottom of the picture.

It's a symbol. And from father's instruction on a few Nephilim symbols, I know how to read it.

I know what it says.

20

I touch the symbol on the wall.

Valkyrie.

Holding up my crystal, I look back into the shadows, back through the rest of the story stretching out before me. The woman is surrounded by animals, leading them, fighting the Nephilim. The woman who stood up against the gatherers and used her powers. The woman who killed a warrior in Valhalla.

I look back at the symbol, my fingers still pressed against its smooth edges. Valkyries were in the Norse myths. According to most mythology, they chose who died in battle and who would have the honor of coming to Valhalla. Of course, the hunters in Valhalla aren't dead—just retired. So perhaps the myths changed over time. Perhaps the term *Valkyrie* means something different to the Norse Nephilim, who inspired the myths. There might have been other bits of truth in the myths—Valkyries with ravens, Valkyries with winged horses, Valkyries with animals of all sorts... Valkyries with the power to kill and to control.

Perhaps this woman was a Valkyrie.

"Fenris," I whisper.

He looks up at me with big golden eyes, his muscular feathered shoulders glinting in the light.

"What if I'm..." I pause and breathe in courage. "What if *I'm* a Valkyrie?"

Fenris simply sits and looks at me, subservient, trusting. Like Moses was. Like the agouti. Like all the animals, even like the centipedes. He waits on my command.

If I really am a Valkyrie...

I can't believe I'm entertaining the thought, but nothing in the recent past has made any sense. None of it. Perhaps I *am* chosen. Perhaps I am more than Soren thinks. Perhaps I am *entirely* different. If I was born with the powers of a Valkyrie, perhaps I was never meant to be a hunter.

A strange sense of relief washes over me. Hunters are the ones who fight and kill. With those strengths, their weakness is too easily succumbing to corruption and darkness. But if I wasn't made to be a fighter, to be a killer—then perhaps the darkness Soren said was inside of me is not such a threat after all.

Except I have killed. I wonder with despair if the woman on the wall ever lost control of her powers and accidentally killed someone. I couldn't control my own power. What if I fail again? What if people die because of me? Because of the darkness inside me and the power I can't seem to control?

I look at the woman on the wall, leading an army. Knowing the full impact of her powers and using them anyway. Knowing what she had to do in the face of darkness.

I think of Aquila, alone in the pit, battling her own darkness and waiting for salvation.

If the strongest hunter I know couldn't defeat the Nephilim...maybe a Valkyrie can.

I swing onto Fenris's back and push my hands deep into his fur. Then I lean forward and whisper into his ear. "Let's go save Aquila."

A door separates us from the main hall. From here, I can hear the drunken singing of hunters, and the scrape of chairs being pushed back as threats and shouting escalate.

Looks like we've arrived just in time. My heart is pounding so fast and hard that it hurts. I close my eyes and try to breathe. And I remember. I'm not alone in this fight. I clutch Fenris and picture the weagles prowling outside the gate. I call their attention, command them to stand at the ready. I can't see them, but I know. My army is waiting.

Then I give Fenris the order.

We burst through the door and soar into the air, flying over the table and all the hunters. Cries and shouts resound below us as the hunters look up.

"It's the girl!"

"She's flying!"

The men below are equal parts surprised and angry, but they are also one hundred percent distracted.

Attack.

The gates heave open, and a flurry of red wings take to the air. Swords are drawn as weagles swoop down, attacking from above. Fenris and I hover over the rest, watching the chaos unfold.

Strike with your talons. Disarm. Push them back. Do not kill them!

I envision everything that must happen, and my army follows. The weagles soar over the hunters' heads, attacking them from behind, pushing them back toward the gates and cornering them. The hunters fight to kill without any hesitation, and some weagles fall, feathers spurting into the air. My heart sinks. This is my fault. And I'm starting to feel drained.

The weagles flounder in confusion as my mental concentration weakens.

You can do this, Norah, I tell myself.

I square my shoulders, and I command the weagles to rise up into the air, away from their attackers. The sounds of battle lessen, and another sound reaches my ears. A squawking sound. I turn to see Freya at the head of the room, stubby arms flapping, beak uselessly issuing complaints. She heaves her rippling weight from side to side, but her legs don't have the strength to take her anywhere.

Soren isn't translating. Isn't standing at her side. It seems he isn't even in the room. I frown, but then I feel relief. Maybe I won't have to fight him after all.

The sound of feet and shouting brings me back to the moment. The hunters surge forward, new weapons in hand. Bows. I gasp as I see what I didn't notice before. Hunters snatching weapons from the walls—the bows and quivers hanging on hooks around the room.

Arrows fill the air around us. I send the weagles diving to disarm the hunters, but many are struck. They're easy targets. My soldiers are falling in front of me, and I don't know what to do. The image of Moses' dead body slumped on the cavern floor rises in my mind. A strange rage fills me.

This has to end.

I direct Fenris toward Freya, and I push him forward. The wind we create pulls against my hair and stings in my eyes, but I am locked on her. And I am not going to relent.

Freya's eyes grow wide, pushing ripples of fat up her forehead, as I come closer and closer, Smite stretched out in front of me.

Just before we collide, I jerk Fenris to the side. Smite swings out and follows, cracking Freya in the side of the head with all the force we've gathered.

She squawks horribly, as though choking. Her head tilts and her body falls to the side, landing on the ground half off the platform. The whole hall shakes. Weagles and hunters alike turn to stare.

Fenris lands on the ground in front of Freya's face. She's blinking in confusion, neck twisted uncomfortably, forcing her to face the ceiling. A curtain of purple blood slides along the back of her head to the ground. Fat squirts out from the impact point, oozing down to the floor. It looks like globs of butter—or worse, worms made out of centipede flesh.

I hear hunters roar behind me, forgetting all about the weagles, as they run to defend their master. Fenris rises up and howls, wings outspread, guarding me from arrows and attackers. But I do not pause. I do not turn.

"You don't know who you're dealing with," I say to Freya, voice dark. She stares up at me with wide, terrified eyes.

I turn to my army.

All eyes are on me. The weagles and the hunters wait. Fenris stands before me, ready to take charge. And I know there is one more thing I have to do.

I hold my hammer over my head and open my mouth to shout. The weagles howl along with me.

Then I raise both arms and send out the command to my army, my helpers. *Chase them out of this hall, up through the tunnels, up to the land of Antarktos.*

Fenris takes to the air first with another howl. And as one body, with more force than I could imagine, the weagles swoop down and drive the hunters toward the gates. Some hunters are scooped up in talons. Some weagles fall to the arrows. But everywhere, Fenris seems to lead, howling, swooping, intimidating. I see fear in many hunters' eyes as they look at the weagles and then at their fallen master. One by one, they turn and flee for the gates.

"Well, well, well," a voice croons behind me.

I recognize that voice.

My stomach curls.

Loki.

I turn to face him in all his ugliness, taking in his red scales and horned head, staring into his evil yellow eyes.

He holds a massive axe at the ready. My distraction makes the weagles pause. Seeing what is about to unfold, the hunters stop, too, though those nearest the door, unaware of the shift, continue to flee.

"You've made quite a mess here." He sneers. "You really have no respect for the great and esteemed hall of Valhalla."

I spit. "And you have no respect for the King's daughter."

"So the princess has found some new slaves," Loki mocks, as he gestures toward the weagles corralling the hunters out of the gates. "I would have thought they'd be a little too savage for your taste."

I grit my teeth. "I defeated your master, demon."

Loki laughs. "The Valkyrie thinks she defeated my master. Isn't that cute?"

I open my mouth to respond, but stop in confusion. Of course I defeated Freya. She's lying on the ground blubbering behind me, unable to pick herself up. And... he called me a Valkyrie.

"What did you say?" I ask, before I can stop myself.

"Valkyrie. One of a disgusting breed of women who has power over the animals of Antarktos." Loki glares at me, but it's demeaning. He's not impressed.

"I control all the animals here." I frown at the pleased look on his face. "And I defeated your master."

Despite the fact that I've said this twice, the grin on his face only grows bigger. And then he speaks.

"You didn't think *she* was the one pulling the strings, did you?"

I look down at Freya, lying bloodied and weak between us. Not healing—at least not visibly. Her beak is still moving, but no sound comes out.

"She's afraid of you." He strokes his chin, though there is no beard there to stroke. I look from him to Freya in her puddle of fat and blood. "She saw you riding that guardian of the gate, and she knew you were a Valkyrie. It's written in Norse mythology. Don't you know?"

My words come slow, uncertain. "I know."

"To her, you are powerful. To me—and to my master— you are filth." Loki spits at my feet. Some of the spatter lands on Freya, who flinches and continues quivering in her mess.

"Who is your master?" I ask.

Loki ignores me and continues his tirade. "You are an abomination of humankind. It was your kind that sent the Nephilim underground and condemned us to hiding for centuries." His hand clasps and unclasps the weapon at his hip. I fight the urge to knock that smile off his face with Smite. Before I do that, I need to know what's really going on here.

"Why aren't you trying to kill me?" I ask.

He smirks. "It is the will of my master, and my master must be obeyed."

"*Who* must be obeyed?"

"Why don't you find out for yourself?" Loki swings an arm backward, gesturing at a door behind Freya's platform. I hadn't noticed it before. It must have been hidden by her massive bulk.

I look at him again, trying to read his features, but I don't find any clues. He's right. I don't know who's pulling the strings here. Not anymore. And it makes me hesitate.

"Don't you want to save your sister?" Loki mocks.

I step onto the platform and move toward the door, looking back over my shoulder. The hall is quiet. The weagles have deferred to me; the hunters to Loki.

I meet Loki's eyes. "You better not play any tricks while I'm gone."

He grins. "I doubt you'll be coming back."

I walk to the door, rest my hand on the handle and breathe deeply.

Then I open it and step inside.

21

The door slams shut behind me, and I am washed in darkness.

My eyes adjust quickly. Too quickly. Once I see where I am, I wish I could go back.

It's my room, my old room in the palace. Spacious and dark, with a bed in the center. My bed.

My throat tightens, and I start to feel like I can't breathe. I take short, shallow breaths, but I can't seem to get enough oxygen. Stars spark in the darkness around me.

I see Soren at the foot of the bed. His thin alien-like lips are peeled back in some sort of grin. His hand rests on the coverlet—my coverlet. My bed. My room with Soren in it, just like it was a year ago.

But there's another person present that wasn't here before.

My sister.

Aquila is tied to the bedpost, blood streaked down her face, her arms and every bit of exposed skin. It looks like she's been beaten mercilessly. Her red hair is a matted nest on her head, sticking out at odd angles and crusty with blood. But while her body is beaten, her eyes are fierce and hard. Animal.

And she's looking at me.

I get the feeling that if she wasn't roped to the bed, she would pounce and tear me apart.

Your sister is mine now, Soren says.

I can't muster up the oxygen for words, so I let the thought broadcast in my mind, knowing he will hear.

You're the master?

Soren laughs, that shredding sound running through my mind. *For someone so smart, you really should have picked up on that sooner.*

His words from the day he threw Aquila and me into the pit run through my mind.

'Freya doesn't need to know.'

Of course. Freya was weak. Freya thought she was in charge, but how much power could she really have? She couldn't move. All she did was give birth and squawk. Soren needed her to provide a big enough figure for the hunters to follow. And he needed the horrible creatures she birthed, hoping to create an army to overthrow my father. But when she couldn't birth anything smart enough to form a sentence, he came up with a new plan. Use the King's daughters to get past the King's defenses. Assassinate him before he knew what happened. And, of course, he had to test the two sisters, to see which one of us could get the job done. When he invaded my mind, he found no traces of a hunter. He probably tested Aquila, too, and erased her memory. But me? He needed to make sure I wouldn't follow and mess up his plan. So he left me with the memories and the terror, thinking I would be too afraid to put up a fight for my sister.

The information enters my mind as though Soren is laying it all out for me to see. He's relishing the opportunity to reveal his power and his plan, I know. I can feel his satisfaction.

But I know something he doesn't. And that knowledge deep inside me is what keeps me from collapsing beneath the fear.

I was enjoying submitting your sister to my will, Soren says. He lifts a long finger and strokes her raw cheek.

Fury swells in my stomach.

So was Loki. He relishes in physical pain. Soren digs his fingernail into an open wound, but Aquila doesn't wince.

Her eyes are fixed on me, furious, hungry. *But I prefer...* His grin grows wider. *Mental pain.* His huge eyes narrow slightly as he focuses on her. She reacts as though he has touched her with a hot iron. She thrashes, rolls her head around in agony and lets out a shriek.

"What are you doing?" I yell.

He chuckles. *Giving her reason to hate you.*

I shudder as I watch my sister's agony, unable to imagine what he must be showing her or saying to her.

"Quil," I whisper. But she can't hear me through the voices in her head.

He stops the mental attack, and Aquila's head slumps. But her eyes roll up to find me, glaring with more hatred than I've ever seen.

We were enjoying our time together before you interrupted, Soren says. *I didn't think you had it in you to fight your way in here.*

"I've got help," I say. And then I realize all my help is out there, behind that door. Fenris is not beside me. Moses is not guarding me. I'm on my own.

Sooner or later she'll be free of these bonds, Soren says, as though he didn't hear me. *And do you know what happens then?*

I stay silent, unwilling to give him a response.

She will teach you true pain. She will fight you until you can't fight anymore. And when you fall, your little army will be free to serve their true master once more. Then she will leave you to starve in the pit.

My voice rasps. "She's my sister. She would never do that."

I know, and Soren knows, that it's a foolish hope. My sister is gone, broken and lost to madness.

Of course, there is another option, he says. *But I know you. You are too much of a coward to do it.*

My throat is dry, and I'm pretty sure I couldn't speak even if I wanted to.

Do what?

Soren tilts his head, his enormous black eyes fixed on me, pulling me into their darkness. *You strike first. You make sure she is too broken to fight. You destroy her, before she can break you.*

I look at my sister's weak body. Her enraged eyes. She is not the sister I recognize, and I know she is not Aquila anymore. She is Aimee, servant of the Nephilim. And I don't know if my sister could ever live in that body again.

Then I look at Soren. He is grinning, waiting for me to fail, lips curled and eyes wide.

I walk toward Aquila. Strike is lying on the floor at her feet, uncurled, dripping with what I'm sure is her blood. I pick it up and turn it over in my hands. I think of the woman on the stone wall with a sword in her hands, the woman with her arms outstretched, the woman who defeated the Nephilim.

I hear Soren's voice in my head again. *You know what you have to do.*

A hunter would obey. A coward would run.

But I am neither.

I am a Valkyrie.

I turn with a speed that neither I nor Soren knew was possible, and thrust the sword between his eyes. I feel a moment of resistance and then it punches through, coming out the back, dripping purple. His eyes widen, but not in pain. It's fear. He heard the words loud and clear, but I repeat them again, out loud this time.

"I am not a hunter," I say, as Soren sinks to the floor. He slides back, and purple blood pools around him. The grin has slipped off his face, and his eyes begin to dull.

"I am a Valkyrie. And I decide who lives and who dies."

Soren's eyes flicker for the last time and then go blank. He's not just dead; he has ceased to exist.

I pull the sword out of his skull and throw it to the ground with a clatter. My head rushes with blood, and I feel dizzy. I killed a Nephilim. I killed a Nephilim *in* Valhalla, where death only comes at the hands of a Valkyrie, like the woman on the wall.

Like me.

Next, I turn to Aquila, dazed, but preparing myself to find a solution. If that means knocking her out until I come up with a way to bring her back, that will have to do. I steel myself and put my hand on Smite, ready for the worst.

But she's not glaring at me. She's quivering and whimpering, eyes on the ground. And she's no longer tied to a bedpost. She's tied to a stake in the ground.

I look around us in shock. The bed is gone. The furniture of my room is gone. All that's left is the post Aquila's tied to and a bunch of crates scattered around the room.

Soren constructed that whole setting in my mind, just to make me afraid.

I shake my head and turn back to my sister.

"Quil?" I whisper, putting a hand under her chin. "It's me. It's Norah."

She looks up at me, her whole body shaking in fear.

"None of what he told you was true," I say. "He's gone now. He can't hurt you anymore."

There's almost no response in her eyes.

I start to work on the knots at her back. As soon as I free her, she collapses to the floor, legs unable to hold her. Some of the blood crusted in her hair flakes away, and I see brown strands beneath. She is either not fully corrupted, or what I saw before was just another of Soren's illusions. I crouch beside her and wrap my arms around her back, careful not to press against the gashes in her skin.

"I'm right here," I say. And I hold her until she stops shaking.

Finally, she looks at me with the barest glimmer of trust in her eyes.

I search for words and find them. "You're Aquila Aimee Vincent, daughter of King Solomon Ull Vincent, ruler of Antarktos. You're strong and brave and fierce. You've faced worse than I could ever imagine and come out still standing. You can defeat these Nephilim. *We* can. I'll be by your side the whole time. And then...then we can go home."

She exhales slowly. I can see her deciding. And then she nods and stands.

I smile and pick her sword up off the floor, wiping it clean on Soren's robe. Then I curl it up and hand it to her. "You'll need this."

She smiles faintly, a little bit of the old Aquila coming to life in her eyes. I start for the door.

"Norah?" she asks, voice soft.

I turn.

"You killed him?" She points at Soren.

I nod, shoulders bowed beneath the weight of what I've done and what I've had to survive. I meet her eyes hesitantly, waiting for her to respond in fear or in disgust.

But there's a small smile on her face. And in her voice, the old joking lilt returns.

"Not so weak after all."

A slow grin spreads over my face. "Nope." I heft Smite from my side and hold it tightly with both hands. "Now let's finish what we started."

22

When we charge into the great hall, the look on Loki's face is priceless. He can't believe his eyes. Two little girls have beaten his master, and I can't help but take time to gloat.

"I believe you said I wouldn't be coming back?"

Loki controls his goggling eyes and responds with anger. "Where's Soren?"

"You have no master." I look at Aquila and smile. She smiles back. "Not anymore."

Loki can't hide his horror. "You—"

"Killed him. You were right—I *am* a Valkyrie. You probably should have warned Soren before I drove a sword through his head."

Loki's eyes narrow in rage.

He lunges at me, axe swinging. I sidestep and turn to face him as he reels, off-balance. Then I aim a blow at his shoulder, but he staggers to the side.

Axe raised, he runs toward me. I stop the axe with Smite, but he keeps pushing, and it takes all my strength to keep it from splitting my head.

Then Aquila jumps in, slicing Loki's arm with her sword. A deep gash opens up along his forearm, and he pulls back, unable to hold the axe up. He turns to her and laughs, seeing the fear in her eyes.

"The hunter is afraid," he mocks. "Did the poor little girl not like Loki's beating?"

Rage fills me. I will not allow him to talk to my sister like that. And I will make sure he never hurts her again.

I swing with all my might and catch him in the stomach. He staggers backward, a stunned look on his face.

The axe clatters to the ground.

"You are a coward," I hiss, walking toward him, Smite outstretched. He takes a few steps back. "You prey on little girls. You hide by disguising yourself as other people. You trick and mock, because you have no real power."

His face creases indignantly and he opens his mouth, as if to retort.

I speak louder. "What will people think when they hear that the great Loki was killed by a twelve-year-old girl? A Valkyrie that you yourself brought into Valhalla to kill whomever she pleased?"

He lunges at me in rage, but he's careless. I slam his feet with Smite. The weight of his body can't be supported by broken toes. He falls on his face. I give him a solid whack to the back of the head. Then another. And a third. When his head is concave and pooling with blood, I stop. His body twitches and stills.

I turn him over, not sure if he is dead. He's unconscious, but still breathing. I pull back my hammer, thinking about all the evil this creature has done, much of it to me, and yet, for a moment, I feel sorry for him. All this time, I thought *I* was the pitiful one. But it is him, and those like him. And for monsters like them, there is no forgiveness. No eternity. No mercy. I bring the hammer down hard, splitting his forehead and ending his long life.

Aquila watches with wide eyes.

"I should probably put Freya out of her misery, too," I say, looking at Freya's flapping stub of an arm. She seems like she's recovered some, and she's trying to stand up. Some sadness seeps into me. Nephilim or not, I never wanted to be a killer. But I am a Valkyrie, and that makes me the only one who can do what must be done.

I end Freya's life quickly, in the same way I ended Loki's.

The hunters have fled the hall, and only a couple of weagles mill around, standing guard. I call them toward us and motion Aquila to one. She stares at me with huge eyes. "What are you doing?" she hisses.

"Flying." I grin. "Just hop on. It's like riding a cresty. Just hold on to its fur."

Aquila climbs onto the weagle's back tentatively, and I mount mine with ease.

"Time to go home," I say. "Let's go."

At my command, the weagles take off. I lead the way. I can tell Aquila is nervous at first—and who wouldn't be shaken up after the trauma she's been through? After a few minutes, she begins to laugh, as the weagle dips through the air and the breeze plays with her hair, pulling more of the blood away. Already I can see the strands of red hair giving way to her natural light brown.

"Do you think Zuh's going crazy with worry?" Aquila calls to me.

I frown. "If she's alive."

We reach the surface faster than I thought possible, bursting into the jungle and then the bright light of day above it. My soul wants to leap with joy, but I can't stop thinking about Zuh.

I look at the unfamiliar terrain all around us. "I don't know which way to go!"

Aquila takes a long look around, glancing once at the sun, getting her bearings, still the better hunter. Then she directs her weagle south. "Follow me!"

Every minute I spend in the sun, I feel my mind and body refreshed. The air is alive and humid, clinging and cleansing. Below, I can hear the sounds of life. Animals squawk and cry out. The jungle teems with life, and as I reach out with my mind, I can feel them all, from the smallest insect to a cresty matriarch hunting for a meal. I'm tempted to reach out and say hello to them all, but Aquila directs her weagle into a downward dive.

"Follow them," I tell Fenris, and we drop from the sky, buffered by extended wings. For a moment I think we'll crash, but with two mighty flaps, Fenris stalls our descent, hovering over a small clearing. It takes a moment for me to recognize it, but all the signs of a struggle with something large are there—broken branches, matted foliage and a lingering stink.

This is where Aquila was taken, but Zuh isn't here.

Remembering that canines have a powerful sense of smell, I take a loop of fabric from my belt. Zuh used to tie her hair up with it. She gave it to me, for my hair, before we set out on our training expedition. I hold the fabric out in front of Fenris's nose and mentally explain what I'd like him to do.

Fenris lands, scours the area with his nose, and then, with a huff, he bolts into the jungle. He has no trouble following the trail that neither I nor Aquila would be able to sniff out after several days and who knows how much rain. After just thirty seconds, we find her. She's leaning against a tree trunk, eyes closed, her dark skin turned pale.

I hop down from Fenris's back and run to my friend's side, Aquila right beside me. I try to steel myself for the worst—she's spent a week in the wilds of Antarktos, injured and alone—but the idea of Zuh being dead nearly undoes me. I can't imagine my life without her steadfast support. We drop to our knees on either side of her. "Zuh!" I shout.

Aquila wraps her fingers around Zuh's limp wrist, checking for a pulse. "She's alive."

Zuh's eyes flutter. "Aquila..."

"I found her, Zuh."

"The Nephilim?" I can tell she's struggling to wake up, the hunter in her demanding she fight. "Loki?"

"Dead," Aquila says. "All of them."

Zuh's hand twitches and then moves. She pats Aquila's hand, smiling slightly.

"It wasn't me," Aquila says.

Just one of Zuh's eyes opens a crack, looking first at Aquila, and then at me. When she sees my grin, her eyebrows rise up. "How?"

I make a sharp squeaking sound, beckoning Fenris. Zuh's still-closed eye pops open when she sees the creature. "I had help."

"But...how?"

"I'm a Valkyrie."

Zuh's eyes flash with recognition. As a young hunter serving the Greeks, she would have never been to Valhalla, but she would have surely heard the stories, including the part played by the first Valkyrie, who commanded animals and helped destroy generations of Nephilim.

Zuh lets out a painful chuckle, winces and then relaxes. "Sounds like you don't need my help anymore."

"We would have never survived without it," Aquila says. "And we still have a lot to learn."

I nod in agreement. "But first we need to take care of you."

While Aquila starts a fire, I call a small centipede from the underground, kill it and start tending to Zuh's now infected wounds. She's strong. With our help, she'll survive. And we'll all walk, or fly, out of the jungle together.

Despite everything that's happened, I feel fresh hope running through me. Hope that Antarktos will see a day where the Nephilim are gone for good. Hope that the hunters chased above ground will find redemption. Hope that Zuh and my sister will heal from their wounds with a story to tell. But most of all, I feel hope because I am not afraid. Because Soren has lost his hold over me forever. Because I know who I am.

Norah Kainda Vincent.
The Last Valkyrie of Antarktos.

ACKNOWLEDGMENTS

First and foremost, I must thank Tori Paquette, who made this co-authoring experience extremely fun. Despite this being her first published book, she handled herself like a pro in every way. From research, to writing style and meeting deadlines. I have little doubt that her career will be long and stunning, and I'm thrilled to be a part of its beginning.

Thanks to Matt Frank and Chris Scalf for their tag-team effort on the cover art, and to Jennifer Larsen, aka: Mayhem's Muse, for modeling. As always, thanks to Kane Gilmour for exceptional edits, Roger Brodeur for detailed proof-reading, along with a great team of advance readers, including Kelly Allenby, Lyn Askew, Sherry Bagley, Julie Carter Cummings, Dustin Dreyling, Donna Fisher, Jamey Lynn Goodyear, Dee Haddrill, Becki Laurent, Jeff Sexton, John Shkor, and Jennifer Turkette.

—Jeremy

ACKNOWLEDGMENTS

First off, I want to thank my parents for encouraging me to write this book, even though it scared me. They have always supported my dream of writing, and they have given me the tools and confidence I needed to pursue that dream.

I want to thank my brother Caleb, who knows the Last Hunter series better than I do, for reading each new scene as I wrote it and keeping me motivated.

I want to thank my friends, especially Aidan for giving me another pair of writer's eyes, Beka for having full confidence that I could accomplish whatever I chose, and all of my new friends at Colby College who have promised to buy this book.

I especially want to thank Jeremy and Hilaree Robinson. Without them, I wouldn't have had this incredible writing opportunity—but more than that, they have been my friends, my mentors, my cheerleaders. Their listening ears, their gentle advice, the beautiful example of their lives, and their unwavering belief in me has influenced my life more than they know.

And thanks, Norah and Aquila, for letting me write about you. I hope you like it.

—Tori

ABOUT THE AUTHORS

Jeremy Robinson is the international bestselling author of over fifty novels and novellas, including *Apocalypse Machine, Island 731*, and *SecondWorld*, as well as the Jack Sigler thriller series and *Project Nemesis*, the highest selling, original (non-licensed) kaiju novel of all time. He's known for mixing elements of science, history and mythology, which has earned him the #1 spot in Science Fiction and Action-Adventure, and secured him as the top creature feature author. Many of his novels have been adapted into comic books, optioned for film and TV, and translated into thirteen languages. He lives in New Hampshire with his wife and three children. Visit him at www.bewareofmonsters.com.

Tori Paquette wrote her first novella when she was thirteen. (No surprise here, but it was a romance story about a princess.) Since then, she has written in as many capacities as possible, including fiction, creative nonfiction, and blogging about mental illness and faith. Her work has been published in *To Write Love On Her Arms*, *Revival Magazine*, and *Delight & Be*, as well as on her own website blog, BoldBrightBeautiful.com. She is a graduate of the Iowa Young Writer's Studio and a student at Colby College, where she is studying creative writing and psychology. Like the real Norah Robinson, Tori is an artist at heart who wants to leave the world more beautiful and more honest than she found it.

COVER DESIGN
STEP BY STEP

The cover for *The Last Valkyrie* was a unique experience. Normally I design covers myself, or on occasion, I hire a single illustrator. But *The Last Valkyrie* is a collaboration between myself and three other people, all of whom did a fantastic job. First is Matt Frank, the artist behind the *Project Nemesis* comic book and tons of Godzilla comics. He penciled the cover, creating the unique composition along with the character and monster looks. Next was model, Jennifer Larson, whose work helped Matt choose the perfect pose for Norah on the cover. Then came Chris Scalf, who digitally painted over the pencils, incorporating Matt's style into a vivid image that is stunning to look at. Finally, with the completed art in hand, I laid out the text. Big thanks to all of you, and I hope we get to work together on more projects!

**STEP 1:
SKETCHES**

**STEP 2:
PHOTO SHOOT**

STEP 3: PENCILS BY MATT FRANK

STEP 4: COLORS BY CHRIS SCALF

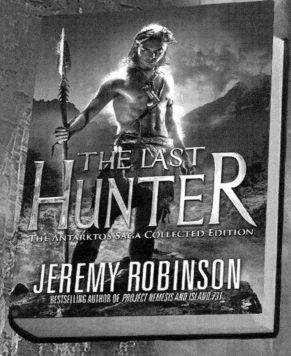

AND THE STORY
THAT STARTED IT ALL

ANTARKTOS
RISING

THE WORLD'S NEWEST CONTINENT IS ALREADY INHABITED

"ANTARKTOS RISING FIRES ON ALL
CYLINDERS IN A SMART, TAUT THRILL."
STEVE BERRY

JEREMY ROBINSON
BESTSELLING AUTHOR OF RAGNAROK AND ISLAND 731

"A NEW DARK CONTINENT OF TERROR."*

ANTARKTOS RISING

* NYT Bestselling Author, James Rollins

40671435R00118

Made in the USA
Middletown, DE
19 February 2017